SANTA CLAUS
SAVES THE WORLD

ROBERT DEVEREAUX

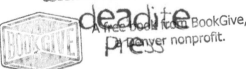

Books Are Essential!

deadite press

A free book from BookGive,
a Denver nonprofit.

www.BookGiveDenver.org

DEADITE PRESS
205 NE BRYANT
PORTLAND, OR 97211
www.DEADITEPRESS.com

AN ERASERHEAD PRESS COMPANY
www.ERASERHEADPRESS.com

ISBN: 978-1-62105-130-5

Printed in the USA.

For Ted,
for Anet and Charley,
for Fred and Maryjo,
and a heavenly host of friends
in the front room not so very long ago.

CHAPTER ONE
THE ASH NYMPH BROODETH

Sing, Goddess, the trials of Saint Nicholas, our at-first-reluctant savior who in the end took on the task of fixing God the Father's rotten botch of a creation, slapdash from the word go, by rejiggering the human psyche.

Sing too, O Lubricious Lady, the Tooth Fairy's store of impotence and frustration, her unbridled delight in her new co-conspirator Venga—exiled from the race of golden girls—and their most ferocious attempts to sink humankind in the bottomless muck and mire of abject depravity.

Neither neglect the hairpin precision—oh let's give it its true name, shall we?—the obsessive-compulsive delivery expertise of that unsexed voyeur, the Easter Bunny, without which expertise this tale would have ended in tragedy.

Finally and not least, sing the hurt and displeasure of the Father God, his estrangement from the Son in favor of the Shame Son got upon the Divine Mother some years past.

Begin then, Sweet Goddess, with an establishing shot of the Tooth Fairy's island, viewing it first from rain-heavy clouds in all its panoramic splendor, then sweeping in upon the former ash nymph as her now dozen imps, come back from their murderous spree on Christmas Eve, finish ravishing her.

Off she throws them, thrilled by their savage assault yet revolted by their stench, their dull-witted ugliness, the vile poison that defines them to the core.

"Scum-sucking sons of a whore," she screamed as she sprang up to reclaim her power, "get you gone!" Her necklace of teeth clattered upon her chest.

Six times she left-and right-fisted the arms of two imps. Six times she starfished them in greasy spangles to far-flung corners of her island.

Into the air she leaped, corkscrewing through ocean waves

to wash their vile spunk from her flesh. Sucking in sea water at her quim, again and again she shot it out in a power douche, killing hapless sea creatures that chanced to swim by. Then, gulping gallon after gallon of ocean, she shat showers of enriched water that drew shimmering schools of fish, growing larger and hardier as they swam through it.

Again airborne, she surveyed her island.

Far off, she spotted the shore where thirteen milk-chocolate eggs from the Divine Mother's breast milk, overlaid with gold leaf, repelled her and her brood.

"Damn them to hell and back!" she said, recalling Santa, his bitch-wife Rachel and her bitch-daughter Wendy, the mewling Easter Bunny, and especially that turncoat motherfucker Chuff, once the butt and scorn of his brother imps, now a token resident at the North Pole.

One day, she vowed, she would reclaim that shore and blast those eggs to smithereens.

Upon the shore she squatted. Through the pelting rain she gazed toward the far horizon, her stiff nipples dripping water on her belly.

She had made the mistake—near daybreak, as she wrapped up her nightly round of bedroom visits—of listening in on what a few brats had said to their bitch-mommies about the coins beneath their pillows.

They held such saccharine notions of her. None had a clue how loathsome they were to her. Greater than her rage at being robbed of her hatred of them upon entering their bedrooms was the rage their notions of her engendered.

One sleepy-eyed cockwielder had blinked up from his pillow at the sow who'd whelped him. "Mommy," he said, "do you think Santa and the Tooth Fairy were here at the same time? I bet they're friends."

"They must be, Timmy. I'm sure of it. But the night is short and they have so many houses to visit. More than likely, they show up at different times. But one thing you can count on. They both love you dearly."

Love little gap-toothed Timmy?

Love the latest roster of snot-nosed brats?

She would have loved to lop their blithering heads off and swallow their skulls for supper.

Had it not been for an intriguing smudge smeared on the horizon, the Tooth Fairy would have indulged her hatred of children for hours.

But that smudge, dark and shiny, beguiled her.

No threat there.

No menace.

Rather, an urgent groin-centered buzz that meant something alluring this way came.

Had she sensed anything to be feared about it, she would have said this thing, whatever it was, traveled at an alarming speed. But what she felt was the speed of delicious anticipation and an urgent desire about to be fulfilled.

CHAPTER TWO
THE WOMB BLURT
OF A NEW BRAT

Speed we now from the raging stewpot of perverse hatred where dwelleth the Tooth Fairy, to the highest heights of heaven itself, indeed to the throne of God the Father, berobed, bebearded, and besotted with a massively majestic ego, the Zeus he once had been—and from time to time became again—ill-concealed beneath His Judeo-Christian veneer.

Afar off, the Son stands observing his father.

Upon the Old Man's lap, mouth to the creator's ear, sits the creature he got upon the Divine Mother when Santa upstaged him by eradicating homophobia—an eradication that seems however to have eroded badly in recent years. Indeed, that brand of hatred has made an ignoble comeback, so entrenched are the ways of man.

The angels refer to him as the Shame Son, since he lacks a name and has refused to take one. As always, the bent-spined runt whispers private words in God's ear. For all the attention the Father pays to anything else, he could be light years away.

More neglected than ever, then, His creation.

A flutter of angel wings.

"You summoned me?"

"I did, Michael," said the Son.

"The usual topic?"

"None other."

"Forgive me, Lord," said the archangel, "but don't you think it's time to let it go?"

"His creation's falling into disrepair. Whenever I try to speak with Him, His attention wanders. Always the Shame Son has His ear, though from the expression on His face, there appear to be equal measures of spite and rage mixed in with the shame."

Michael simply listened, not commenting, offering no commiseration.

The Son nodded. "I know. There's nothing to be done. This has to run its course, whatever that might be. But meanwhile the creation continues to devolve toward ruin. And there's only so much we onlookers can do."

"That's right."

The Son loved this archangel above all, the former trickster god Hermes who trod carefully now, aware of his shortcomings and his tendency to act, without intending to, in ways that led to all sorts of mischief, even unto disaster.

"But don't you think," continued Michael, "your time would be far better spent surveying the world and . . . hold on, I'm being summoned."

"So you are." The Son's gaze shot earthward, taking in the summoner's degree of upset. "Do you mind if I go along? I think I'll be needed."

Michael's eyes reflected hints of doubt. The thought flickered that the Son might mistrust his judgment in such matters. But that doubt vanished. They weren't, after all, mortals. No need to conceal anything here. The Son would have shared whatever doubts he felt.

"I don't mind at all," said Michael. "Wendy's quite upset. Our visit is bound to comfort her. Let's be off."

The Son took one last mournful glance at his father and sped away, Michael hard on his heels.

Post-delivery, after the long night's assembly line restocking of Santa's pack to keep it replenished on his rounds, the elves were fully engaged in play.

The North Pole's snowy commons were all a-jangle with jinglebells. Everywhere appeared a riotous smear of bright green jerkins, caps, and slippers, slippers that magically defied the snow's melt despite deep drifts—soft, sunlit, and white as doves—everywhere.

The elves were in high spirits this year, dashing and darting about, quick-flung snowballs hurtling through the air to find unfailingly their mark.

In the distance stood Gregor at the half-door of his stables, an eternal grump on his face, his arms folded in stern disapproval

9

of all he saw. Though the others were far too wrapped up in fun to pay him much heed, they harbored nothing but kind wishes toward him, holding out always the hope that one day he would ease into a smile, soften, cease at last all judgment, give up his ridiculous and utterly transparent desire—though he imagined they were fooled—to overthrow Santa and take control.

What a shock it would be to see Gregor smile.

Anya and Rachel watched from the cottage porch, Santa's older wife in her festive red and green dress, the younger in mittens, leggings, down pants, and a down jacket. Rachel, though immortal and therefore immune from cold, was partial to the winter clothing she had worn as a mortal. Christmas felt somehow more genuine that way.

Rachel sensed an unusual degree of mischief in the air. Many elves were exchanging covert glances. Even Chuff, the Tooth Fairy's reformed imp, seemed part of some conspiracy.

"Fritz and Herbert are in on it," said Anya, pointing them out to Rachel.

Snowball and Nightwind leapt onto the railings, their scandalized eyes taking in the revelry, their tails flicking in feline outrage.

"So I noticed," said Rachel. "Josef and Englebert as well. They've really found their playful sides since they left their brother and moved into the dormitory."

"Gregor misses them."

"We should bring the old grouch some chocolate cupcakes or apricot scones sometime, topped with a dash of kindly advice." Rachel laughed. "Not that he'd take it, but you never know. No one can say when such a seed might germinate."

Anya nodded into the commons. "Here we go!"

A few hundred elves—Chuff too—winked out into magic time, abruptly thinning the ranks. The others stopped, glanced about in confusion, and laughed it off, ready to resume their sprints, taunts, and tumbles through the snow.

Out of the north woods emerged most of the elves that had vanished, Fritz, Herbert, and Chuff in the lead. On their shoulders they hefted what might have been an immense table top or the Jolly Green Giant's front door, a massive oak plank nearly two feet thick and more than a hundred feet in length. Under great weight they staggered, but kept steady on.

Another set of elves, obeying the barked orders of Knecht Rupert and the close-up maneuvering of his backward-walking sidekicks Johann the Elder and Gustav, rolled a metal drum—forty feet tall, were it stood up—straight to the center of the commons, where Santa and Anya had once made love to the great gold coin, turning it into an immortal Rachel and foiling the Tooth Fairy's revenge upon Santa.

Anya gasped. "Why, it's a—"

The elves who hadn't been in on the secret caught on at the same moment. They let free with whoops of delight, tossing their caps high in the air and catching them as they jangled down.

"Yes indeed," said Rachel.

The cats, as usual, were scandalized and didn't mind showing it.

Those rolling the drum placed it just so and stepped clear of it. The table top that wasn't a table top moved over the drum, inches above but not touching it, and was quickly secured to it with L-shaped brackets and massive screws, elves busy from below and above.

The others eagerly crowded about, choosing up sides in no particular order.

When the work was done, the play began.

Stepladders appeared, though many of Santa's helpers were too impatient for that and took a running leap onto one side or the other.

The thing teetered one way, tottered the other.

Shouts arose. Those hopping on board urged new companions to join them, until the balance righted itself and they began triumphantly to sink. Then it was the turn of their brothers across the center line—once exultant, now playfully panicking—to recruit more weight for their side.

So it went. The wood groaned and the platform threatened to buckle, as hundreds of elves piled on, crowding together, some falling off the edges into the snow and scrambling to return.

11

Finally, when it was clear that the team on the right had the advantage, several renegade mischief makers on the left banded together and made a massive rush across the center line to the right, dragging Chuff with them.

Chuff's greater bulk sealed the bargain.

Suddenly the teeter-totter's right side sank to the snow, lofting the left side abruptly skyward.

Catapulted through the air, the elves on the left curved in laughing green arcs as they sailed above their triumphant brothers, tumbling downward into the drifts. Their joy was buried in snow, only to spring forth like new-grown shoots.

"Again!" they shouted.

The winners abandoned ship and a new set of initial contenders broke into teams to begin anew.

It occurred to Rachel to wonder where Santa and Wendy had got to. No matter, she thought. They're often elsewhere for a spell, always rejoining the festivities eventually.

Soon she was once more absorbed—as were Anya, Nightwind, and Snowball—in the unfolding spectacle of delicate balances, tipping points, shouts of anguish and triumph, and green elfin arcs brilliant with jingle and glee, painted across a bright blue sky.

She could have shot into the rain and raced across the ocean to meet whatever now sped toward her. But for once—though it struck her as odd—she longed to be possessed and penetrated by something powerful and in charge.

Her breathing went ragged.

As the smudge drew near, it grew more distinct. A creature of scales approached, its skin mottled black and silver, its head hidden beneath the waves.

All around her, voices sighed and sang, so faint she might have imagined them.

The voices of her sisters!

Long dead those nymphs, mowed down in slaughter during the Great Transformation even as she made her foolish pact with Zeus and traded a life of riotous sensual indulgence for an insatiable craving for teeth, her trivialization into a rug rat's monstrous dream, a slave to endless visits to bedrooms, her digestive tract a grotesque money-spewing machine. They had had such grand times together, she and her sisters, with the rough-furred, thick-cocked satyrs who probed and poked them, parry and thrust, who matched them lust for lust in never-ending attempts to top every climax with the next, while the heady scent of pine and oak filled their nostrils.

Save for the pine nymph Pitys, Santa's now-nearly-wizened main squeeze, all of them had gone down in screams and torment.

Of all the wood nymphs, she had been fondest of the Hamadryads, daughters of Oxylus and Hamadryas. Huddled in frenzy, they had suffered a thousand cruel cuts: the touch-needy Balanos; Kraneia, ever in heat; cunt-lovely Karya, redolent of hazelnut; Morea of the mulberry; Aigeiros, pressed against the black poplar; the bark-licking elm nymph Ptelea; Ampelos of the vines, ample of breast and buttock; and much favored as a lover, Syke of the fig tree, soft, lush, and savory on the tongue.

Bringing them to mind typically drove the Tooth Fairy into paroxysms of unquenchable rage and desire, blasting the heavens and that sky-god bastard Zeus with her impotent harangues. But now, the stomach-churning memories of their slaughter joined those beguiling wisps of song to welcome the beast that undulated through a white-capped sea.

Its speed redoubled.

Massively ugly its horned head.

So swift it came on, with such a headlong rush, that the ocean parted on each side. Across the sand it shot and twisted tight about her, layer on layer of its body oozing and flowing over her.

It should have repelled her into resistance.

But she surrendered willingly to its thrall.

The serpent defied all logic. It held her in the tightest of bonds, even as those bonds slipped and slithered across her flesh. Desire exploded in her mind, to be at once fulfilled and replaced by new desire.

Touched, tossed, and caressed, she surrendered to its

13

embrace, her limbs broken and restored, genital thrusts too many to count sinking into every exposed place on her body.

Time stopped.

Time hurtled onward.

Time held no meaning.

Pleasure unlike any she had ever known swept her into a frenzy of bleats and bellows, her mind shattered and gone.

When consciousness returned, she lay alone and full-bellied on the beach, a fetus swelling inside her, pressing against bladder and bowel, gaping wide her vulva and gushing forth with a bloody blurt.

A fourteenth imp shot out, sprouting full-grown in an instant.

But unlike the others—seeded from thirteen strikes of Zeus's thunderbolts, spewed from her seared cunt to vex her with their dull, slope-headed desire—this boy-child beguiled right out of the gate.

Though he was as repulsive as his brothers—blunt-browed, stoop-shouldered, three-fingered, with the stench of rotting fish about him—a beguiling beauty nonetheless graced his ugliness. He seemed encased in a dime-thin coating of flexible ice. His sex thrust up boldly, ghastly but enticing, oozing krill oil along the length of its shaft, flushing her healed quim with fluid, quickening her breath from trot to canter.

His eyes burned coolly into hers.

"Hello, Mother," he said in honeyed tones, a deep bass-baritone that seduced and thrilled.

"Come here," she said.

"Not yet."

Before she could counter him, he lifted a hand as if to touch her with his icy fingers.

Instead, his fingers veered off and thrust downward toward Tartarus, summoning some distant thing even as his eyes continued to enthrall her.

CHAPTER THREE
SANTA COOLS, CRISIS HEATS UP

As his elves' gleeful shouts echoed in the commons, Saint Nicholas, considerably slimmed down from our last look at him, sat cross-legged in his office on the plush burgundy cushion master weaver Ludwig had made after Santa's triumph over homophobia.

Long gone and buried was the Coke machine that had dominated the space where the jolly old elf sat.

Dear reader, I wish I could tell you that Santa Claus, fresh from his Christmas Eve deliveries, was as fired up as ever, his thoughts turned to preparing for the year of toy making ahead.

For centuries that had been his way, bursting always with enthusiasm, his generosity unbounded, eager to create new delights for well-behaved children despite having just delivered gifts to tens of millions of homes the night before.

But you deserve the unvarnished truth.

No sugarcoating, then. Neither hem nor haw.

Truth is, Saint Nicholas was one unhappy elf.

To be more precise, a scarcely discernible hint of unhappiness hung about him, though I assure you it ran very deep indeed.

Years before, he and Wendy had eagerly embraced their new Thanksgiving task: to single out a handful of grown-up mortals gone bad—sweet Jesus, were there any other kind?—and set them on proper paths in a series of evening visits.

But those sorties came nowhere close, neither in impact nor in magnitude, to that of their fight against homophobia.

More infuriating, human beings had proven highly resistant to change—bounders, backsliders, slaves to moral inertia. The most daring fix to their problems seemed temporary at best.

As for homophobia, it had slowly crept back into this stinking race of rotters, a damnable part of the massive weave

15

of errors and misjudgments, fears and follies, which befouled their lives. What had appeared at first a decisive victory had deteriorated over the years into no victory at all. One might almost think that God had actively undone that triumph.

Santa Claus had always avoided grown-ups, much preferring to focus on the innocence of children.

But this annual contact with naughty grown-ups, a novelty still, threatened to tarnish even his love for their offspring.

He glanced at the thick tome resting on its special podium in one corner of the office. Bound in black leather, this magical book was constantly updating its contents, always the same combined thickness though the Naughty section was invariably thicker by far than the Nice. A few hours before his deliveries, he would wink into magic time and use the Nice pages to plan his itinerary, never pausing, until recently, to wonder why Ginny Smith or Ryan O'Fallon had shifted into the book's Naughty section.

Now, God help him, he regarded every child's name found in the Nice section with suspicion.

How long before thumbsucking Lizzie Meeks from Greenwood, South Carolina would succumb to this or that character flaw and bid farewell to her innocence forever?

How many years before giggling trike-rider Ethan Vane of Austin, Texas fell before schoolyard bullies, grew sullen, and shifted direction, his moral compass never again pointing true north?

Santa's mind began listing them, their homes, their notes beside milk and cookies, the occasional carrots for his reindeer, the scent of their Christmas trees still fresh in his nostrils.

No, he thought. I will not obsess over them. I will not anticipate their fates, not think the worst of them, when the best—most likely unsustainable (God damn it to hell!)—comes as quickly to mind.

Finally, there was the small matter of his Pan side, pretty much integrated and settled into submission.

Not entirely, though.

Mortals in trouble, his and Wendy's Thanksgiving targets, often meant *female* mortals in trouble.

The satyr in him wanted to ravish every last one of them, to make her sweat, pant, and scream, hit her top notes of ecstasy, ease down into bedded bliss, and be ready to go again in an instant. Outward beauty or its lack mattered not at all to him. Neither did the perfection or imperfection of her thoughts, words, and deeds.

His goatish lusts begged for attention.

The mind inside his horned head itched and burned, brimming with desire to touch them, taste them, take them, make them laugh and gasp, gape and swoon, and scream unto death at his erotic skill.

Those desires, though inwardly rampant, were firmly squelched and never, God help him, acted upon.

His Santa persona was in charge now, generosity triumphing over Pan's bestial urges.

But were there weaknesses the Pan in him might exploit? Could an irreversible shift in power ensue?

There were, and it could.

Never quite secure, then, his triumph.

More like keeping a respectful vigil.

More like observing.

Not eradicating Pan. Just hearing the same stories over and over, refusing to judge them, allowing them to wallow in erotic melodrama without being tempted to act upon them.

Santa sighed.

There were days when meditation without agitation was simply not in the cards.

Time to give it up, rejoin his elves in the commons, and lose himself in snowball fights and being whipped off the tail end of a long, green, ice-skating snake.

Fritz and Herbert chose that moment to rap at his office door.

"Come in, lads, come in," he called out. "Enter and welcome!"

"What the—?" said Venga.

One moment, the great god Hades was pressing the heat and heft of his prick against her thigh, fingering her moist, gold-leafed flower like Midas inventorying his treasures. Persephone in a sheer gown looked on, waiting her turn.

The next, an invisible force wrenched her from the depths of Tartarus. Through the Underworld she shot, passing through earth and sea, cannonballing out of the ocean floor through a turbulence of white caps to clatter in a heap upon the shores of the Tooth Fairy's island. She rose as majestically as she could, a tabby brushing off a fall as of no consequence.

Savoring the miracle of fresh air and the zesty churn of ocean after an eternity in the confines of Hades' domain, she instantly recognized the ash nymph who stood before her. From the savagery in her eyes, it was clear that Adrasteia had never lost herself in her Tooth Fairy identity.

Beside Adrasteia slouched an imp whose radiance made Venga gasp.

"Mother," he said, pointing to Venga, "meet your new helper."

"Fuck if I will—"

But the imp stilled her with a raised hand.

This set Adrasteia to boiling.

She tried to seize him but failed again and again. When her hand shot out, he was always elsewhere.

"May I introduce myself?" he said to Venga in the midst of his mad shifts. "I'm Quint, the latest addition to this ferocious lady's brood."

"I gather you know my name," said Venga.

"I do."

Adrasteia steamed. "Tell me what this is about. And what this gold-plated whore is doing here uninvited."

"Of course, Mother," Quint said.

Then he told the Tooth Fairy who Venga was, how she had come to be in the Underworld, and how she could help achieve her dreams of conquest.

The Tooth Fairy brightened, though she remained wary. Her resolve seemed to Venga to harden. Plans blossomed in her brain. Still, her wall of distrust did not come down.

"Gronk!"

Instantly a hideous imp flew in—flailing from his mother's

18

psychic tug—to tumble abjectly before her.

"Buzz off to the North Pole," said the Tooth Fairy. "Check out any new-hatched plans to save the human race, look in on your fuckwad brother Chuff and that grumbler Gregor—both of them exploitable points of weakness—and report back at once."

"Yes, Mother," groveled Gronk, glancing at Venga. "Who's this?"

"Stop wasting time!"

She landed a kick on Gronk's misshapen buttocks. Up he shot into the sky, bumbling northward.

"I'll shadow him," said Quint. "I may see things he can't."

Venga could tell that Adrasteia had mixed feelings about Quint's boldness. Some mother-son rule on this island was being violated.

But a look of lust rose on the ash nymph's face as she watched her newest son fly off, lust fueled by a smoldering core of anger.

She started to finger herself.

"I can help with that," said Venga, moving in for a turn with this savage creature. The pent-up rage, the heights of passion, the violence of her every thought, word, and deed—all of these promised a very lovely time indeed. And there wasn't the least hint of rebuff in the ash nymph's reaction, just a do-what-you-dare sassiness.

Venga caught the scent of Adrasteia's juices, sharp, sweet, savory, and mouthwatering.

Tastier even than Persephone, this one!

After Wendy shocked the archangel Michael with what she had to show him (the Son feigned surprise, but nothing ever surprised him), she shut off the vile spigot of the vision and restored quiet and sanity to her bedroom. Michael defluttered his wings and gave her a look of compassion. "It might be a good idea to show this to Santa Claus."

In earlier times she might have objected, hoping from a wide-eyed innocence to spare her stepfather any unpleasantness.

But the past dozen years had sobered and matured her. In looking for mortals to reform at Thanksgiving, a task Santa had been quick to delegate to her, she had cast her gaze with greater care into the future of the human beings under consideration.

No longer, narrow projections of the coming good fortune of the hundred exceptional boys and girls she treated to sleigh rides on Christmas Eve. Now she saw, sober and up close, the horrendous missteps of the misguided, their squandered potential for good, the wounds both deliberate and thoughtless that grown-ups inflicted upon one another and upon children as well.

And she had honed her ability to pick out patterns in the societal sweep, to highlight and to track them into the future.

Moreover, she had made it a point to study human history through books and DVDs and by attending to the words of gifted professors at university lecterns.

She had learned about and absorbed to the bone the many highs and the far more numerous lows in the recorded history of this peculiar creature collectively known as humankind.

Gut-wrenching, the things she had witnessed. The devolution of a species whose evolutionary reach had only sporadically been tried.

And now this.

Wendy peered out her front window as the elves frolicked in the commons. She rapped on the glass to catch the attention of Heinrich, the six dollmakers whose centuries sleeping together and working side by side had made them nearly identical. They came to the front door, their high, tight voices releasing—like newborn skylarks—the day's joy from their long black beards.

"Yes, Heinrich, it is indeed a wondrous Christmas Day. Merry Christmas to you all! Now would you be so kind as to ask Fritz and Herbert to come at once? It's very important."

"Of course, dear Wendy."

Away they scurried, beelining for the skating pond, from which direction soon emerged the two friends, Santa's favorite helper Fritz, and Herbert the expert blesser and cameramaker.

Another quick exchange of pleasantries.

Another summons.

Then they were off, headed toward the workshop to fetch her stepfather.

Santa walked between Fritz and Herbert, joking with them, fending off random volleys of snowballs from hopped-up clusters of elves, and hearing how deliveries had gone from the perspective of those working at this end of the operation.

As smooth as ever, they said, though mishaps and glitches had as usual to be handled along the way.

The gingerbread house gave off a warm glow, a hint of divinity enfolding them as they drew near.

"After you, dear friends," said Santa.

"Oh but Wendy asked for you only," Fritz objected.

"Bless her heart," said Herbert.

"Another time, then."

They took their leave, running into a renewed hail of snowballs and kicking up snow fluffs as they went.

Santa followed the glow to Wendy's bedroom, guessing correctly that she had heavenly visitors.

He knew she confided often in Michael.

Beside the archangel stood the Son.

Happiness, however, seemed in short supply.

Wendy's face was tinged with despair. "Daddy, I need to show you something."

Damned human race run amuck again.

What else could it be?

"Go ahead, dear. I'm steeled for the worst."

"First," she said, "next year, I'm seeing dramatic shifts in the length of your Naughty and Nice lists. And far worse shifts every Christmas to come."

She unveiled her evidence, those familiar sections of his book of judgments widening and thinning as never before.

"I focused on broader patterns of human behavior, seeking an explanation for the upsurge in naughty children. I found it, all right."

Then she opened up the vision, ugly, wide, coming nearer

day by day, poised to pour forth a panoply of horrors. And what horrors they were.

Before them, in an infinite space on Wendy's wall, from a starting point decades before, the months ahead unrolled.

Santa knew of course that naughty grown-ups, both young and old, performed many unworthy acts every day. There wasn't a second that wasn't choked with them.

But what Wendy revealed in sickening detail was a pattern of upsurge that gathered steam, darkening as it changed. The rate of unkind words and deeds had markedly increased. The meanness of spirit too. And outpourings from a ravenous media which held the globe in its cash-fed death grip.

They saw it all on an instant, the coming hell on earth and the series of hellish deeds strung out and accelerating toward it.

At one point, Wendy begged the Savior to soften the edges. He did so, the words and thoughts blurred, the acts robbed of their vividness.

Until the final moments.

Then came crescendos of hurt, killing, judgment, fears hooking them, unworthy unkindnesses, out for themselves, cynicism fed and magnified by electronic amplifiers.

In the final moments, there was a horrific deluge of self-inflicted wrath. The Son looked distraught. Santa and Michael were close to tears.

"Observe, Daddy. Do you see the sudden upsweep of nastiness near the end?"

Santa felt faint. "I do."

"Now look at Valentine's Day. Frank Worthington of Ames, Iowa will choose that day to dump his wife and children in favor of bunny-boiler Laura Bowles. That's the tipping point."

"It's terrible what he's doing there," said Santa. "An innocent lad not so very long ago, that boy. But his act seems not as grandiose or decisive as a murder or a . . . well, as any number of sins far more heinous than calling quits to a marriage."

"Agreed," said Wendy. "But he happens, with this act, to push humankind over the edge. Tipping points work that way.

Things become exponentially worse for everyone all at once, with no turning back."

She shut off the vision then. Silence returned, like a hammer blow, to the bedroom.

Wendy said through her sobs, "Something has to be done before it's too late."

Santa found it hard to breathe, hard to find the right words, and—what was worse—hard to know what he and his elves could do to stop the imminent disaster in store for the human race.

The Easter Bunny woke to the distant rumble of multicolored eggs rumping and rolling along narrow, wooden troughs.

His eyelids lifted to let in the dawn.

As always since helping Santa and Wendy eradicate homophobia—but, oh my, that seemed, did it not, to be doggedly creeping back?—his first view on waking was of the knapsack hanging on one wall, a divine ray of sunshine illuminating it, though no other part of his underground burrow was similarly lit and there was no natural light source in evidence.

His little miracle.

A reminder of the day he had delivered chocolate eggs made from the Divine Mother's milk.

He so loved his life, filled as it was with three joys: The memory of his most recent delivery of eggs and candy. The anticipation of deliveries to come, the squeals of happiness from youngsters on Easter egg hunts, rummaging through their baskets for candy corn, biting off the ears (ouch!) of chocolate bunnies. And watching mortals copulate, skin to skin, mouth to mouth, mouth to sex organs, such a wonder to behold, to see, to smell, to imagine touching it all—and with a tweak of his nose to grant impregnation to those who ardently wished it.

Yesterday, his nose twitch had helped conjoin the zygotes of Hermann and Hilda Behrens in Berlin as they enjoyed mask play, latex costumes, and whips and chains in their little mockup of a dungeon. So cute that pair.

23

And in Cairo, the wriggle of his nose had helped an unusually modest couple, Badru and Irisi Chalthoum, to their fourth incipient bun in the oven. Not perhaps the wisest choice given their impoverished state, but then who was he to judge?

Any moment now, he would stir, rouse himself, and careen madly about to kickstart the life force in him.

He would look in on his vast store of layers, take in the sweet stench of chickens, the incessant dropping of ovoid wonders from their rumps, the soft contented sounds of cluck and murmur. In the distance, he would hear the creation and cutting of fake green grass, and farther back the automated manufacture of baskets.

Then—

What in heaven's name was this?

A fist gripped him in the pit of his stomach.

Barely noticeable at first.

Then gradually commanding his attention.

But what was it?

A premonition of . . . something.

Odd.

Could it be that his next delivery—if it happened at all (but how could that be?)—was doomed to thread through a landscape of humankind unlike any he had experienced before?

Surely not.

Then why this clutch at his belly? Why the waning urge to race joyfully about his burrow?

Instead, a terrible paralysis held him.

The knapsack caught his eye then, a slow dimming of the sunlight at its edges until it began to fade into the earthen walls of the burrow. At once the sunlight returned. But its loss for even a second was enough to strike terror in his heart.

He settled down.

No call to be alarmed.

Delusion, surely.

Time enough to wake to the day.

For now, he ought to grab further sleep, throw off his premonitions, and start the day afresh.

CHAPTER FOUR
HOW PSYCHES ARE MADE

"Come with me," said the Son.

"Oh, my!" exclaimed Santa and Wendy let out a shout of exultation.

Up they rose, swift and motorized as hummingbirds, passing through the protective bubble around their community, sweeping aside the driving snow, straight through the thinning atmosphere and the floor of the Empyrean. The Son led the way, followed by Michael, with Santa and Wendy in the warmth of their wake.

An eyeblink and they found themselves before the gates of a vast building, its top vanishing beyond the power of immortal sight, so wide to left and right that it exceeded the limits of either horizon.

"Oh, my!" repeated Santa, having closed the gape of his mouth and wrapped a protective arm about his stepdaughter. Shaking with terror and delight, Wendy took comfort in him.

Michael to the Son: "Why bring them here?"

The Son stilled him with a raised hand.

"Welcome," he said, "to the psyche factory."

Abruptly they were inside, high up, looking down from the face of a towering chronometer, a huge yet soundless grandfather clock. Below, two tiny figures toiled at a long workbench, one seated, one standing. Assisting them was a vast array of females fashioned of gold, svelte, naked, beguiling Santa's eye without doing anything to spark his desires.

Each golden girl floating in from the right held a bright half-sphere of multicolored energy, a dome that grew from baseball- to beachball-sized as she approached the workbench.

She gave it to the female figure, who held it briefly in her prayerful hands and passed it to the male, a swarthy blacksmith laboring near a wide hole in the workbench. From that hole arose the lower half of a sphere, an inverted dome. With skill long honed and attention undivided he affixed one dome to the other, his expert hands moving to connect them in hundreds of places.

Each female floating up on the left carried away a complete sphere, now bristling with energy. This too, by the time the female had drifted far enough from the workbench, could be carried in the palm of her hand and shrunk to even smaller dimensions as she disappeared in the distance.

The soft glow of magic time was unmistakable.

It evidently glowed here always, surrounding this work environment and the immortals constantly at play in it.

Though built on a monumental scale, the building held Santa and Wendy with the bosomy warmth of a grandmother—close, confiding, comforting, every appetite satisfied without being overindulged.

Then they were abruptly standing on the floor, no startle on anyone's part, as inevitable this meeting as their next breath.

No swoop down. No movement at all.

They were simply there before the couple, Michael and the Son beside them.

Santa's attention was first captivated by the male, burly, ugly, hunched over his work, his legs broken but well-balanced in elaborate gold servomechanisms, his beard wild and unkempt, his eyes ferocious and fiery yet rich with compassion.

"My dear Dionysus," he asked the Son with a growl that caressed, sparks of delight in his gaze, "to what do we owe the pleasure?"

Santa's eye strayed to the female of the couple, at once fixing on her to the exclusion of all else.

In the distance, the Son was saying, "Santa, may I introduce Hephaestus."

The growler laughed. "What would be the point? Our renowned satyr king no longer gives a tinker's damn about *me*. He's thunderstruck by my wife, as is everyone. But this fellow has fallen hard indeed."

To Santa's ears, the rough sounds held no meaning. The

goddess who stood before him engaged all of his senses. Pan craved her without mercy, leaping to lust fulfillment in image after image that put paid to Santa's all-consuming generosity. She showed little more than a hint of her beauty, the rest muted lest madness claim the looker-on.

"Call me Aphrodite," she said.

Her voice, a low flute that caressed and captivated, brought Santa to his knees in further crumble. She was full-on lovable and in that moment he loved her to the end of time.

Far more than lust, then, this attraction.

And not the limerance that bamboozles human beings into projecting their desires onto a mate at first meeting.

But he knew he had to control it, to stay away from her, to avert his eyes—lest Pan subvert Santa quite.

"That's better," said Hephaestus. "My beloved is a looker, all right, though some have done more than look. Delighted to meet you, Saint Nicholas, for so I shall call you. And you are—?"

"Wendy. Santa's my stepdad. May I ask what you're doing?"

He deflected the question to his wife. "Dear?"

"We prepare the souls of newborns, assisted by our golden girls," said Aphrodite, nodding to the robotic women. "Hephaestus made them ages ago. We also archive the spent souls of the dead, about a quarter million each day."

The melody of that voice cut straight to Santa's heart, enthralling and blissfully sirenic.

"The under-psyche is standard issue," continued Aphrodite. "The over-psyches are unique, organically grown in the factory's upper reaches. It's our job to couple them so that the complete soul is ready at the infant's first breath." She gestured toward the one her husband was completing. "Just a pinch of love to seal the joins and this one is on its way."

"You're beautiful," said Wendy.

"Thank you, sweetheart. I was made, for the most part, essentially irresistible."

"Mind if I take a peek?" said Santa, fascinated by the intricacy of the psyche halves.

"Not at all." Hephaestus halted the line of golden females and granted him a closer look at the under-psyche.

God's creation.

A thing of majesty and marvel, yet—

Santa could tell at once that it was a hastily thrown together botch job. There was much of magnificence to it, much to admire and marvel over. But it was as if the creator's mind had wandered at some point—at many, to be honest—and grown careless. Weaknesses galore dwelt within. Temptability, disconnects, misconnects, beguiling dead ends where talent and time could be quickly and irrevocably squandered, treacherous pools of laziness and sloth, fight-or-flight areas where fear and anger could swiftly establish beachheads.

In short, a divine mess.

Said the Son, "That's why I wanted you to see this."

"I don't understand."

"Let me be direct. Would you be willing to fix the under-psyche, shore it up where weak, add new parts and mechanisms that encourage worthy tendencies, make easier and more selectable the humane paths, harder and less enticing the inhumane ones?"

"Please say yes, Daddy," said Wendy.

"Not so fast, love," said Santa. "Is this approved of from on high? Assuming, that is, I can find the will to set aside my distaste for fallen mortals and entertain this notion even for an instant?"

"Let me check." The Son vanished.

"Gone to ask permission," said Michael.

"Permission?" said Santa in alarm. "That's a bit premature."

"If you don't mind. . . ." Hephaestus signaled his assembly line to restart and resumed his work. His expert hands danced above the latest newly formed sphere of lights and gizmos.

No longer secure upon the right hand of God—that position having been usurped twelve years before—the Son had kept his distance, observing the Shame Son sitting on God's lap and whispering in His ear.

Now the Son drew near.

The heads of the collusive pair turned as one, their eyes locking on his approach.

Heavenly unease.

"Apologies, Father," he said. "It's a matter of some urgency, else I'd leave you be."

No reply. The faintest tightening of the crow's feet at the corners of the Father's eyes spoke all the reply that was required.

"I'll be brief. Humanity is fast approaching a crisis point."

God's gaze shifted almost beyond perception.

"Yes, Father, I know You know. I've asked Santa if he and his elves might be interested in tinkering with the under-psyche. Shoring it up. Revamping a few spots here and there. Really a major overhaul, but I'm sure they're up to it. They did so well with the scourge of homophobia. They're efficient. They're thorough. We couldn't ask for more expert reengineering."

The Son gestured downward. "Observe." At once the coming disaster unfolded before them in all its horrors.

The Father hadn't bothered to look. He just kept staring at the Son.

"The good Saint Nick is reluctant. I thought I'd seek Your permission so I could assure him on that point at least. You can see why, I think. It's a major task, he has major distractibility as regards Aphrodite, he's adult-phobic, and he feels—wrongly, in my view—that he'd be out of his league."

God glared. The Shame Son looked both shocked and violated. That's *his* problem, thought the Son.

"I'll interrupt no longer. Just give me your assent."

Not a stir of that great bearded face.

But with utmost respect and with the firm resolve that urgency brings, the Son stood his ground.

Then it came.

Not an outburst of wrath.

Not a dismissive wave.

No thunderbolts.

Just the nod of His head, so slight that anyone but the Son might have missed it.

29

"Good then," he said and drifted backward to his usual distance.

Staring eyes unlocked.

The enthroned figures resumed their obscene parody of Madonna and Child, enveloped not in motherly love but in divine inadequacy, shame, and demotion.

Sped then the Son to the heavenly psyche factory, bent on convincing Saint Nick to take on the task proposed to him.

"I'm back," said the Son. "God assents."

"Now wait," objected Santa. "With all the usual tasks on my plate, you're asking me to improve the human psyche?"

"Not improve. Re-create from the ground up. And only the under-psyche, not the whole thing."

Santa was sorely tempted.

But the temptation to tinker with the human psyche wasn't his only temptation.

"There isn't enough time. I've spent my entire life avoiding even the *thought* of an adult mortal. Give me good little boys and girls every time. They delight me. They keep me young."

Aphrodite stood beside Hephaestus, effortlessly beaming forth every variety of love as she blessed the next over-psyche, passed it to her mate, and looked with love upon the completed psyche passing out of his hands.

Impossible.

But perhaps in this vast building was a place where he and his elves could work alone and unencumbered, out of her presence.

Said the Son, "Granted you'll be seeing some awful places, the worst possible areas of disappointment, so bad I'm sure they slipped by my Father at the time He created the under-psyche. But this is your chance to fix all that, to infuse the human soul with the worthiest tendencies—under my tutelage if you like."

But was the rottenness truly an accident? Or had Zeus modeled humankind on himself, failings at all?

That was the crux.

There was no way he'd be able to keep to his best qualities

only. He could tap into Santa's generosity, warmth, and kindness. But Pan would be there too, sometimes boldly in evidence, sometimes lurking in the shadows.

Could he stand being directly responsible for yet another botched creation? This time, if he failed, the naughty side of humankind would be traceable to him alone.

Inspiration.

"I like the idea of your tutelage. Wendy has shown us what's in store for mortals if nothing is done. So I guess the question is, could I or my helpers reshape things for the better and thereby avert the impending tragedy?"

"I'm sure of it."

"And if we fail, if there are still problems with the human psyche, could this be an ongoing effort?"

"That I'm not so sure about."

Not the answer he expected.

Something occurred to him.

"Is there no chance that God Himself could do this, and with far less effort?"

"Just a sec." The Son winked out, then winked back in, chastened. "None."

Rock and a hard place.

Santa perused the under-psyche on the workbench. Magnificent. Dreadful. A tinkerer's temptation. The urge was practically sexual. Then Aphrodite—or his fuckworthy projection upon her—invaded his mind.

I can't do this. I'll fail. Grown-ups will be even worse than they are now.

Aphrodite, Aphrodite, Aphrodite.

"Yes," he said, "with provisos."

Wendy let out a squeal of delight. Michael and the Son looked relieved.

"So as not to disturb these two, we'll need our own work area. I'll put my best elves on this. I'll supervise them but I'll not touch these psyches myself. My focus shall remain preparations for next Christmas. I'll look in every now and then. And we'll need an easy way for my helpers to pass between heaven and the North Pole."

31

"Not a problem, that last," said the Son.

"No?"

"Come with me."

He gestured and there were at once a new set of doors in the wall before them, ornate, carved, and painted holly-berry red and ivy green.

"Michael, lead the way."

The archangel rose into the air, spread his hands, and the doors began to open.

CHAPTER FIVE
UNEXPECTED SKEWS
AND CURVEBALLS

Krista Worthington ran out of patience with Frank again.

A bumbler in the kitchen, indecisive in any and all matters of choice, he all too easily got on her nerves, and seemed smugly content—even to a smirk—with provoking her.

"Too many cooks," she said.

"Okay, okay. I'll set the table, feed the cat, throw together a salad."

"Check the greens, okay? If they've gone over, just use Romaine. And this time, go easy on the chopped apricots."

Frank tetched at her. "I know how to make a salad."

Wrong. He forgot every damned time.

But Krista caught herself. She left untouched the knives she might have thrown at him.

Not that it helped. He could read her every mood, just as she could his.

Did every marriage blither down eventually to such idiotic bickering?

They loved and adored their kids Maggie and Sam.

These days, her favorite Frank moments occurred as he carried Sam against his chest on walks through the neighborhood and read Roald Dahl classics to Maggie tucked tight in her bed, her eyes wide upon visions of giant peaches and crushed mean aunties.

But her husband's work stressed him out, carried no rewards worth the name, and left him exhausted and distracted. He spent too much time on the net, doing God knows what with God knows whom.

They had been so perfectly mated.

Now, she wasn't so sure. She knew he had to be feeling the same, perhaps even acting on it.

Day in, day out—drop the kids at school or daycare, go to

work (him software, her retail sales at Pier One), come home, perform a dreary set of brain dumps on each other, play with the kids, then read—or in Frank's case hit the laptop.

It was time to confide in her mother.

If only she weren't so far away.

That night, the Tooth Fairy tested her limits once more, foolishly thinking her repeated efforts would eventually erode those limits.

Soon, she thought, she would be able to carry her hatred across every bedroom threshold on her route, ever nearer the bed, and finally to the sleeping child itself—no longer having to content herself with eating one tiny little tooth, but able finally to deskeletonize every rug rat, leave behind deboned husks of muscle and skin, and pile up heaps of filthy lucre on the bed to console Mommy and Daddy.

Her hatred reached its height in the home of Sally and Ken Falco on the outskirts of Detroit. She swept down before their modest duplex, ready to savage little Ginny Mae Falco in her bed.

The night blew wild and windy.

The Tooth Fairy's necklace of teeth smacked against her chest, her nipples stiff with rage.

Through the locked front door she flew, zooming up the stairs intent on murder. In a heartbeat, she would enter the bedroom and go in for the kill, Ginny Mae's pillow-pressed tooth mere dessert after a main course of skull and bones. And once she had breached the dam behind which Zeus had for centuries imprisoned her, there would be no stopping her reign of terror.

Nothing but tiny corpses in bedrooms across the globe.

Breeders the world over would quickly catch on, burying baby teeth in backyards as soon as they fell out. But myths are slow to die and human stupidity is long-lasting. There would always be clueless parents, as well as those who didn't believe in her at all. There would always be brats, greedy for coins beneath their morning pillows, brats who hid those critical moments of dental trauma from their wised-up parents.

Besides, if her imps could go out marauding, why then so could she.

The bedroom door loomed up, bathed in the glow of a Mickey Mouse nightlight in the hall. She passed through it as if it were smoke.

But the moment she entered Ginny Mae's bedroom, her fireball of ferocity sucked down tight inside, held there by ungodly hands. That accursed, sickly sweet, not-like-her-at-all persona rose to the fore.

There lay the girl, thick blond hair riotous on her pillow, her mouth lolled open, tormenting the Tooth Fairy with its sampler of teeth.

Deep inside, she craved to pry apart the little girl's jaw, tear out the gleaming white kernels, and cram them down her throat as Ginny Mae started up from sleep, her wailing lips burbling blood. She would rip the simpering rug rat open and yank out her bones, watching her suffer and die.

But those feelings remained buried inside.

Heavy upon her and in control arose some damned species of kindness, every gesture genuine, caring, and counter to the darkness in her heart. Whenever she caught this unreal façade in a bedroom mirror, she cursed its every move.

Yet she was powerless to stop it.

Her hand slid beneath Ginny Mae's pillow. A baby tooth lay there, caked blood at its base. She gulped it down, felt it shift inside, curved a hand along her left buttock to her anus, and palmed a quick poot of half a dozen Roosevelt dimes.

As she slid the coins beneath the child's pillow, an obscene blessing passed her lips. "May God and His angels watch over you, darling Ginny Mae, protecting you from all harm."

What a mockery those words were!

She left the room, eager to drop the mask of good. Once in the hallway, her hatred sprang forth as bold and all-consuming as ever.

She turned back to the door, ready to smash it.

But her fist halted a hair's breadth from the wood. Had she been human, the rush of air alone might have splintered it.

A vivid image of Pan surged up.

Rough sex in the woods. Her face bruised beneath his hairy fist. His fuck-flesh shoved up hard inside her, rousing her passion with his own.

That image gave way to an image of his new self, the saint who was no saint at all, fucking her in a hut hidden in the woods. Or beside his hag-wife as she lay suspended outside magic time, the soft brush of Pan's beard electric on the Tooth Fairy's cheek as he danced her like a rag doll below.

Then abrupt abandonment.

And for what?

For some sorry little mortal cunt, Rachel the bitch's name, turned immortal by Zeus's intervention after the Tooth Fairy had swallowed her whole and shat her out as a giant gold coin.

Pan would pay for that.

He had already paid for it.

But his debt to her would never diminish.

Not until Pan shook the Santa shit out of his head, brought his lust once more to the fore, threw his two simpering wives out, and replaced them with her—not until then would she be satisfied.

She pressed against the bedroom door, her lips on the veneer. "Fuck you, Ginny Mae Falco. May your life be one unending series of miseries and heartaches!"

Then she wheeled and was gone.

Chuff showed up right on cue.

Stupid dumb fuck, thought Gregor.

What drew the imp to the stables every damned day? A touch of gluttony and a perverse fondness for reindeer food, as well as an inexplicable need to pat every last one of them between the antlers while he cooed fond nothings into their furry little ears.

No matter.

Chuff was thick-headed, slow to even *begin* to take Gregor's hints.

But he was, after all, one of the Tooth Fairy's imps, a former murderer of misbehaving kids in his past life. And reformed sinners were notorious backsliders, at least in the human arena.

"Come on in, son," said Gregor. "Frolicking in the snow takes a lot out of you, I'm sure. Fuel up. Lucifer and the others have already chowed down and are snoozing. Note Comet and Cupid's bloated bellies, the greedy little beasties! For you, my dear Chuff, I've prepared an extra-large helping of berries, willow buds, and aspen shoots."

"Yum!" Chuff's eyes lit up and he set to.

Neither took note of the two invisible, inaudible, unsniffable imps floating near the stable ceiling and catching every word.

"That's right. Scarf it down. Of all of Santa's helpers, you're my favorite. Even above my brothers, who once slept here but abandoned me when I failed to topple Saint Nick from the seat of power. A couple of Cains they are, a couple of turncoat wretches!"

Through a mouthful, the imp said, "Gregor is good to me. Santa Claus is good to me. Who would want to topple him? A rotten thing to want, no?"

Stifling the urge to harrumph at the little idiot, Gregor did his best to emit a kind-hearted chuckle, though it sounded more like a belched growl.

"Not at all. Santa's fine as far as he goes, but that's not far enough. There's too much jolly about him. His discipline sags. Under his leadership, such as it is, his troops have devolved into a gaggle of lackadaisical scatterwits.

"Eat up, Chuff, eat up!

"Moreover, there's something not quite right about him. A host of secrets in his past. Something really peculiar happened here about twenty years ago, but I'm damned if I can recall what. It has to do with his wife Anya and all of the elves except me. I held my head high. I refused to . . . well, that's where memory fails. I have no idea what I refused to do.

"All I know is, that refusal lifts me morally head and shoulders above Mister Not-Quite-Pristine Jolly Old Elf. I deserve his power. I deserve his house, his sleigh, his cushy office. His women, come to that. Why should that freaking bowl-full-of-jelly get to bump up against the otter-sleek tummies of *two* wives, while no elf has even one wife? Ask yourself that!"

Chuff looked doubtful. "Gregor mad?"

"No need to fear, dear boy. I just get easily worked up. Injustice does that to a body. So what do you say? Are you in? Will you help with the toppling?"

"That wouldn't be nice, Gregor. Not nice at all. So, no, you do whatever toppling you like. Chuff will go on helping with the heavy lifting. Can Chuff pet the reindeer now?"

Patience. Patience. Hold it in, don't let it show.

"Did Gregor hear Chuff?"

"Oh yes, Gregor heard Chuff."

Lose the sarcasm. Just keep working on him. Drip by drip. And one day, the final drip would wear down the dolt's resistance.

"If you're very gentle and don't wake them, you can give each one a little pat. All finished eating?"

"Yes, sir. Oh, yes, sir."

Gregor put a guiding hand on the imp's bent spine and steered him toward the stalls.

"Gronk, old buddy, I think we have all we need," said Quint, pressed against the stable ceiling.

He began to speed off, Gronk bumbling behind.

But Quint was brought up short at the sight of a modest little building just off the commons near the elves' dormitory, a building that hadn't existed when they'd arrived a half hour before. It boasted a simple grandeur and was fashioned of the most magnificent cuts of rosewood, ornate yet not ostentatious.

Two tall doors began to open in it. Bright red and green they were and intricately carved.

"Hold up, Gronk. This looks interesting."

Still cloaked in invisibility, they arrived at the new building just as the archangel Michael led Santa and Wendy out into the commons, followed by no less a figure than the Son of God.

"We're home!" said Wendy in surprise.

Santa looked confused. "I don't quite—"

"The psyche factory coexists here and in heaven," said the

38

Son. "That's how the Father wanted things. Anyone working on the under-psyche may enter by this door. No need for long trips. Easy access to the tools and advice you and your elves might need."

"Come on. " Quint grabbed Gronk and shoved him through the door to size things up—the huge vaulted space, two immortals bent over a workbench, a steady stream of golden girls, the half-spheres they gave the crippled god, the full spheres they took from him. "I think Mom'll find this fascinating."

"Hey, the robots look just like what's her name."

"Sharp eyes, Gronk, old buddy. But let's catch what Saint Nick's saying."

Back out they flew. Clusters of elves had begun to gather in respectful awe sufficiently distant not to invade the privacy of Santa, Wendy, the Son, and the archangel Michael, yet near enough to satisfy their urge to gawk.

Many had doffed their hats.

All stood silent or kept their whispers brief.

Now Santa's wives joined him, and Gronk watched as the jolly old elf briefed them, then bade farewell to the heavenly immortals as they vanished, and turned to address his workers.

CHAPTER SIX
A NEW TASK AT THE NORTH POLE

Here goes nothing, thought Santa, steeling himself for likely disaster ahead.

"Beloved friends," he said, "we have been charged with a task unlike anything we have done before. Pray, gather about."

With the utmost efficiency, they streamed in close.

Softly to Rachel and Anya, "Can we really succeed at this?"

"Of course we can, Claus," said Anya.

Love shone in Rachel's eyes. "No question about it."

Beaming, Santa turned to his helpers. "My dear companions and colleagues, sharers in the divine work of gifting well-behaved boys and girls, I have always regarded this fine and worthy community as a heaven on earth.

"Well, now we literally have a slice of heaven in our midst. This is the psyche factory in which new mortal souls are first brought into existence and in which a mirrored copy of each one is archived. This building exists here and in heaven as well. All of you chosen to work in it will be in both places at once.

"I note your puzzled looks. What purpose does this building serve us at the North Pole? What task am I talking about? And to what do we owe the blessing of those heavenly visitors?"

Santa looked out over the snowy commons, the sun brilliant on the rolling drifts yet not at all blinding to immortal eyes. All it took was to commune with these dear souls and his worries receded, his Pan side hushed.

He had been asked to do the impossible.

Yet at this moment he knew that it was possible, it could be done, and that it would indeed be done, no matter what obstacles stood in their way.

"My dear friends, the human race has never been a shining example of perfection. The joys of childhood are too often forgotten as they age, as they succumb to rage and rottenness, to scarcity models in how they choose to live, to guile and to ridiculously grandiose views of themselves.

"Today, humankind is headed toward irreversible horrors if nothing is done to avert them. If we fail to act, there may never *be* another Christmas, at least none we would recognize as the magical holiday we have always devoted ourselves to.

"We have been given the chance to re-engineer the under-psyche common to all mortals, and Wendy and I have seized upon that chance.

"Time is short, the task complex. Our firm deadline is Valentine's Day. No slippage allowed. And failure is not an option.

"Wendy and I have seen the under-psyche up close. Those who love to tinker, who are up to an impossible challenge—and that would be every last one of you—will itch to dig in and correct the multitude of flaws that plague this mechanism.

"Even as we devote our finest efforts to this critical work, we must continue building our inventory of toys toward next December twenty-fifth. I'll give my usual pep talk tomorrow morning in the workshop. And I will as always supervise those efforts.

"I ask Rachel to oversee this new task, bringing her management skills to bear. Fritz, Herbert, and Ludwig, if they would be so kind as to accept the appointment, will spearhead the engineering effort."

Santa picked them out in the crowd and saw from the elation on their faces that whatever he suggested they would gladly accept. Ludwig, through his squint, looked puzzled and skeptical, but there was no hiding his pride at being chosen.

"Make no mistake, dearly beloveds: This is extra work for many of us, under intense pressure, and the stakes couldn't be higher.

"But we are up to the task. We must succeed, and grandly. There is no other option. With heavenly help, we *shall* succeed. Are you with me, lads?"

The shouts of affirmation were deafening, the bells on the caps lofted into the air jingling as one.

A grand moment, thought Santa.

Then: *Good God, what a treacherous quagmire I've stepped into!*

When Quint and Gronk bumbled back to the Tooth Fairy's island, she and Venga were still at each other in ways that looked more like a fight to the death than an erotic embrace.

"Hold off," she shouted at the newcomers, casting a look of lust at Quint. Then, springing forward, she took a huge bite out of Venga's left breast. The gold flesh instantly healed and she spat her torn gobbet, dripping with ichor, onto the shore.

Venga fisted a hank of hair, yanked back on it—the Tooth Fairy's neck bones cracking—and slammed her lips onto the exposed flesh, raising a huge welt on her throat. So fierce was her suction that the ash nymph's windpipe collapsed like a sucked-out straw.

Then they broke free of one another, panting more from exhaustion than arousal, and fell to the sand.

She glared at her offspring. "Report!"

Quint's eardrums hurt and for a moment his normal speech sounded to him whispered. "You're not going to believe what Pan's up to now."

"Cut the crap, sonny boy."

Quint launched into the details. His mother drank them in, along with his permanent, majestic arousal, not hurrying him along with jabs or questions, almost as though she had stopped caring about grabbing power from Pan or Zeus.

Venga listened with a look of stunned delight.

As Quint spoke, Gronk nodded like an idiot, saying, "Yep, yep," at odd intervals.

"You see now," Quint finished, "why I brought you out of Hades."

"Indeed," said Venga.

"All right, Little Miss Golden Shit-Eater," said the Tooth Fairy. "Spill the beans."

Venga complied. "It's like this. I hated Hephaestus with

42

a passion. I was just one of his damned serving wenches, a handmaiden and nothing more. So once I'd homed in on what he was doing and how he was doing it, I broke from the line.

"I'm through, I told myself. Let my twin Frippa and the others convey half-domes to the immortal smith and carry off new-created psyches to the archives.

"My life path lay elsewhere.

"I'd overheard Aphrodite mention an inner sanctum where the psyches of immortals were kept. I mucked about, searching for it. Weren't no policing up there, no such nonsense, so I took what time I needed and had no fear of being discovered.

"Eventually I found the divine stash of psyches, all of them from the lowliest angel to the Sky God himself, clearly labeled.

"For a moment, I dallied over my own psyche. Don't be a fool, I thought. You don't want to change yours and make an irreversible mistake.

"Then I took down the psyche of Zeburiel, one of the sixty-four angelic wardens of the seven heavenly halls. I assumed a minor shift in his behavior would never be noticed.

"But as soon as I attempted a change, I found myself thrown from heaven, out of control as I fell. The air tore at my golden skin as through the distance from heaven to earth and down smack into the ground I went, continuing on to Tartarus and into the waiting arms of Hades.

"Someone—Zeus probably or one of his minions—had fully informed the God of the Underworld, who told me as he raped me that there was no escaping my fate, that heaven was off limits to me—and, glory be to the great god Zeus, wasn't my cunt the tastiest little slice of cherry pie it had been his pleasure to violate.

"Motherfucking pig!

"Now I'm free of him, I'm here, and nobody ever said the North Pole was off limits. I burn to test my theory, to sneak back into the psyche factory and do undetected what I started to do ages ago."

Through it all, Quint watched his mother. Her face was unreadable. "Are you finished?" she asked.

"I am."

"Well," said the Tooth Fairy, "we are *far* from finished, we four conspirators. We've just begun. There are plans that need hatching, all kinds of mischief to be set upon the world. Let's get to it."

And to it they got.

God the Father knew of course that His Son approached, knew what he would say when he arrived, knew the whole course of their conversation, the Son's retreat, and the sarcasm-laden exchange He would have with His younger son sitting on His lap, pouring shame into His ear.

But the Father was also superb at forgetting, from one nanosecond to the next. Nothing like instant déjà vu to kill spontaneity. And life was best lived, even His life, as a series of surprises.

So He suffered His no-longer-only-begotten son to draw near, bow obeisance, extend a heartfelt and oh-so-nonjudgmental greeting to his brother, open his divine yap, and say, "Father, Santa Claus has agreed to take on the task we spoke of. The psyche factory now stands, as You requested, in two places—"

"Yes, yes. Anything else?"

"I beg permission to help him in any way I can."

Give 'em an inch, they take a light year.

He stared at His offspring, aching to bite his blessed head off. Ever kind and caring, a splendid role model goddammit, no hint of ego, a fully realized being on earth and up here, longsuffering and in perfect love with his suffering. The soft-hearted little fuck had a cross to bear and loved bearing it.

Now here he was mucking about with the heart of his father's creation, daring to question its perfection, drawing a power-hungry, lust-obsessed Pan into his plans.

"Permission granted."

Just enough rope.

"Thank you, Father." And with a nod to his brother and one more insufferable bow, the former Dionysus was off and away.

"Dipping My wick into Mary's honeypot way back when was, I'm afraid, a mistake."

"A terrible lapse in judgment," said the Shame Son, "though what a piece she was."

"The joker who just left descended, made wise, told a boatload of parables, defied nature now and then to impress the rubes, tangled with politicians—always a fatal error, that—and managed to get himself nailed to a cross. Not even coming back from the dead had the desired effect.

"He failed.

"When I say he failed, we're talking major fuckup here. I let him run the show. Barely a generation went by before they began lying about him, what he said, what he did. And soon after, they started laying the groundwork for power grabs and repressions, stoking fears, channeling money and adulation their way. They killed in his name, put him on a pedestal, forced those who didn't believe in their goddamned dogma to toe the line or die. The list goes on."

The little fellow on his lap raised the wisp of a smile. "A major fuckup indeed."

"Yes, and now he goes after another shot—not the Second Coming, we'll save that for later—a chance to queer the deal again, to make things worse, to intend good but deliver evil.

"You and I, we're going to sit here and enjoy the show. If nothing else, it has entertainment value.

"Let them try, say I. Let them tinker, from here to hell and back, with the under-psyche. Good luck and fuck you, say I. Muck with My perfect creation, damn you, you'll suffer the consequences."

The Shame Son sighed. "Such a waste of energy. I see regret and shame in their futures. 'Tis folly to be wise where ignorance is bliss."

"Now there was a mortal!"

"Maybe you should have withheld permission."

The Father smiled wickedly. "Maybe you're wrong."

CHAPTER SEVEN
ELFIN ROLES REDEFINED
AND FACTORED IN

After Santa's annual pep talk in the workshop the next
morning, he brought Fritz, Herbert, and Ludwig up front,
Rachel as well, and addressed the crowd.

"This is going to be a busy year, especially these next two
months. We can't afford to fall behind in creating new toys,
sleds, dolls, bikes, what have you, for next Christmas. Even
granted access to magic time, it's all we can do to keep up
with demand.

"But Rachel will be guiding these three good souls, and
many of you most likely, in reshaping the human under-
psyche, with a deadline of Valentine's Day, a deadline that
cannot slip.

"We're going to be strapped.

"But your spirits, no matter the task, always shine through—
focused, positive, cheerful, able to head off problems. Stay on
course, say I. Stoke those reserves, be elflike in all things, and
we shall not fail."

Santa surveyed his blessed crew, no better band of workers
imaginable, nay, not even the heavenly host, dare he say it.

"A show of hands please, which of you is willing to
volunteer some time toward this effort?"

Santa smiled.

"God bless you all, every last one of you. Fritz, Herbert,
Ludwig, please choose an initial hundred now."

The three elves huddled.

Then, taking Santa's place at the lectern, Fritz reeled off
the hundred names, gesturing to each of them as he did so. He
spoke with dispatch, yet each name upon his lips sang with
history and affection.

"Knecht Rupert.

"Johann the Elder.

"Gustav.

"Friedrich.

"Franz the watchmaker."

With each name, the one chosen yelped with joy, peeled off, and moved to the front of assembly.

When he had finished, Rachel took over. Santa fell in love with her all over again, so strong and assured, so lovely in body and soul.

"Thanks, Fritz," she said. "No time like the present to orient ourselves. So I ask this initial crew to follow me into the psyche factory. Let's go!"

She led them out of the workshop, waving back at her husband as she went.

"The rest of you," said Santa, "kindly assume your posts and attend to the business at hand. This will be, I have no doubt, the best Christmas ever!"

But Pan crept to the windows of his soul, pressed his nose against the glass, and stared unblinking to beat the band.

That raised the hackles on Santa's neck.

From a crossbeam in the stable, Quint and Gronk listened in on the oceanic outpourings of Gregor's blather. Except for the reindeer, he was alone and muttering to beat the band.

The grumpiest elf was always entertaining, thought Quint. If anyone at the North Pole might be recruited to help the Tooth Fairy's efforts, it was Gregor.

Now he was pacing like a panther, spewing insane desires in every direction. "Damned jolly old son of a bitch, unworthy of his position. Somehow I got stuck as a stable boy, hoodwinked into believing it would be an honor to serve Saint Nicholas thus. For too short a time in the battle against nosepicking, swooping in beneath Santa's notice, I tasted power. I crave more. No one's more deserving than I. Voices in my dreams tell me so and it's true."

"Does he talk in his sleep?" Quint asked Gronk. "While you're squatting on his chest and pumping up his megalomania, I mean?"

"Nope. Just scrunches up his face."

Lightbulb.

"You know what?" said Quint. "You ought to turn visible. See what happens."

"Would that be smart?"

"He's not the whistleblower sort. What's the worst? He might freak out, yell at you to buzz off. But if he's accommodating, you may win him over. It's worth a try."

Quint had a bit more convincing to do. But before long, Gronk bumbled down and eased off the mantle of invisibility such that a vague shadow grew gradual substance and Gregor's eyes widened. He stopped his pacing and stood dumbfounded.

"Call me Gronk. It's my name."

Gregor glared at him. "Who the hell are you?"

"Chuff's brother. The oldest of the Tooth Fairy's sons. And quite possibly your friend."

Quint saw that Gregor was hooked, though he put up quite a struggle before he got to yes.

And for all of Gronk's numbnuts stupidity, the imp had beguilement down pat. Call it animal cunning.

When Gronk spoke of squatting on the chests of sleeping elves and pouring trouble into their ears, Gregor—was it possible?—broke into the hint of a smile, the first Quint had seen on his scowling puss.

"Do you do that to Santa too? You don't? Oh you must start tonight. Undermine his resolve. He has issues. I know it. Magnify them, whatever they are."

And into a new rant Gregor launched, holding forth for a solid hour, Gronk unable to get a word in.

Quint sat above, enjoying the show.

Fritz had never passed from one wonder to another in so short a time.

Even if he had entered the psyche factory with his eyes closed, he would have felt himself stepping into heaven, the embrace of blessings warmly enveloping him. But his eyes were wide open.

And as he and his brother elves followed Rachel inside, the vast intimacy of the space made him gasp. Its limitless loft and breadth made him feel not small but towering, both in height and in capabilities.

A golden V rose to either side of the two immortals toiling at the long workbench. Then he saw that this V was made of golden goddesses—tall, leggy, without clothing, variably tressed, strong, assured, and quite captivating. They steadily descended from the right, each carrying an over-psyche. Each over-psyche was shot through with light, complex yet simple in design, worked into uniqueness and untapped potential.

Rising on the left, the golden goddesses carried off the completed psyches, ascending into infinitude.

"Welcome," said the crippled smith seated at the workbench. "You'll work over yonder." At his gesture, a more compact work area sprang up soundlessly, a workbench modeled after his, with many stools at the ready.

Herbert gasped.

Fritz wondered at his friend's astonishment. Their future work area was impressive, to be sure, but not enough to provoke such a response. Then he saw that Herbert was staring at the speaker's companion, who stood on the smith's left. Fritz knew her instantly as Aphrodite, Goddess of Love.

She revealed the hundredth part of a hundredth part of herself, yet it stopped them in their tracks.

"Cover up, darling," said her male consort. "Your beauty is drowning out my words."

At once she dimmed to prosaic dullness.

"Follow me, my friends." He rose painfully from his workbench and made his way to the new one, carrying his latest fully formed psyche.

There he set it down, and though it was spherical, it did not move from where he had placed it.

"First lesson: Watch what I do. It's not hard. Note how my fingers move and shift about this psyche. And now, out of it comes . . . a clone."

Right beside it, a duplicate appeared.

The god tossed the original over his shoulder to the waiting golden girl at his workbench.

"Feel free, any of you, to go into our archives, which

Aphrodite will show you now, clone the psyche of any human being, living or dead, and bring it back here to work on. Any change made to the clone occurs in the original as well, though Aphrodite will teach you how to back out your changes at any time.

"One thing more. Eons ago, I created these golden girls as willing helpers. Avail yourselves of them."

'Excuse me, sir," Ludwig piped up. "What tools do we use and what exactly are we to do? I weave cloth. That's my specialty. I don't see where I come in."

The crippled god dismissed him: "Not my concern."

"Don't worry, Ludwig," said Rachel. "We're coming to that."

Hephaestus went on. "All I do is assemble the new ones and speed them on their way. Your fool's errand is your own. You want my opinion? Fixing the human psyche is as thankless and impossible a task as trying to turn this broken body of mine into an Adonis. Good luck, say I, and Zeus help you."

With a wave of his hand, he dismissed them and hobbled back to his station. "Okay, ladies, resume production."

Poor fellow, thought Fritz.

With mounting eagerness, he followed Aphrodite's diaphanous drift across the marble floor toward what new wonders awaited them.

CHAPTER EIGHT
ELUSIVE PSYCHES AND A
BUDDING BLASTED ROMANCE

"Be not alarmed," said Fritz as Frank Worthington, he of the tipping point, materialized before him and Ludwig. On the workbench sat a clone of the mortal's psyche.

But Worthington was indeed freaked out and made it loudly known. "Holy fucking Jesus!" he said. "Who the hell are you guys supposed to be? Keebler elves or something?"

Then he caught a whiff of pine needles, softened, and grew calm. "I must be—"

"You're not drunk. Not crazy either," Ludwig said.

"How do you feel about Krista?" asked Fritz, staring into the mortal's psyche and giving the mortal himself a side glance only.

"My wife is none of your goddamned business."

"Kind sir, please answer the question."

Worthington was thrown off balance. "She'll do."

Fritz noted which parts of the mortal's psyche lit up and what color they were. More to the point, he felt into the emotions they carried.

He pumped up the love and generosity toward the man's wife, while undermining the defenses against her Worthington had thrown up over the years. Then he gestured to overlay the psyche inside the man.

"How do you feel toward her now?"

"What did you just do? Are you trying some kind of mind control or something?"

"Answer, please."

"Damned if I will. What the hell are you doing to me? And what is this place? If you're part of Santa Claus's operation, where's his workshop? Where are the toys, the reindeer, the sleigh, the whole nine yards? And what," he asked, pointing at his psyche, "is that thing?"

51

No matter what Fritz and Ludwig said, Worthington remained hopping mad and refused to cooperate.

Finally, they restored his psyche, wiped clean his memory, and returned him to earth.

Ludwig squinted and let out a sigh. "That guy Frank? He's one tough cookie. We may have to alter our methodology a bit, don't you think, Fritz? Check with Saint Nick, see what he says."

"Indeed," said Fritz. "The blacksmith too."

The Tooth Fairy wondered where Quint went when he retired for the night. From his first day, he refused to fraternize with the others, and none of them had any idea where he disappeared to.

One day while Quint and Gronk were off spying at the North Pole, the Tooth Fairy took the opportunity of thoroughly exploring her realm, keeping her brats otherwise occupied so as not to rouse their curiosity.

It was none of their business if she lusted after her new son and wanted to sniff out on his ways.

Finally, persistence paid off.

A stray gleam of miniscule gold coins near the base of the mountain by a seldom traveled stretch of sand gave the place away. Each coin was so small, it fit on a fingertip. So thin, the lightest wind blew it off.

A generous trail of them led her behind boulders to a cave she had never known existed.

And inside that cave, she found a mass of treasure impossible to credit. By itself, each pile of coins—of many sizes, shapes, and metals—was unimpressive. But there were so many of them, and Quint had been with her for such a short time, that she was at a loss to explain so vast a quantity of lucre, not to mention the scattering of tiny gold coins dribbled on the sand near them.

Money excited her, of course. Not a surprise, given her manner of turning teeth into coins.

But there was something particularly enticing about this hoard of money. It glowed in so beguiling a way, giving off a light of its own. And it had almost a loamy scent, an aroma that lit up the pleasure centers of her brain.

This would bear further investigation.

Though its presence aroused her mightily, it also stoked her fury at Quint's impudence. She wanted to collar him and demand answers. This was her realm. She was in charge. The discovery that Quint had kept such secrets burrowed deep into her skin and made it burn.

Carefully erasing all trace of her having been there, the Tooth Fairy decided for the moment to keep her own counsel.

Recriminations and countermeasures would keep.

Night time at the North Pole.

The elves were snoring away in the dormitory. Saint Nick lay between Anya and Rachel, the three of them lost in dreamland after hours of delicious lovemaking. Wendy slept soundly in her gingerbread house.

A perfect time for Venga to steal into their domain, clone a psyche or two, and escape undetected.

Quint had schooled her thoroughly on the location of the psyche factory, the precise manner Hephaestus used to clone human souls, and the hours when it was least likely that anyone was about.

He had also told her that Gregor rarely slept, that his bed remained precisely made up for much of the night, and that at the half-door to the stables he kept an eagle eye on the commons under moonlight.

"He's ours, right?"

"So it would seem."

"I'll find out."

Thus, bolder than brass, Venga decided to make her first foray into forbidden territory by landing near the stable, making eye contact with the surprised Gregor, raising a finger to her lips, and sashaying boldly past him on her way to the factory.

Not bad, she thought.

A ballsy, gutsy sort of guy. Ugly and grumpy in the extreme, a goddamn glowering grouch through and through.

But so what? There was real spirit there. Real spunk. Meat one could sink one's teeth into.

A calm winter's night.

No breeze, no chill.

Just moonlit snowdrifts, centuries-old buildings that maintained themselves, and tall, scented evergreens randoming off in all directions.

A paradise for immortals engaged in bringing joy to little boys and girls—before each child's inevitable fall into moral corruption, failing health, disappointments, recriminations, shaky connections, inept governance, botched opportunities at magnanimity, and the whole sorry ball of wax that made for mortal adulthood.

Venga slipped through the double doors into the factory's outer chamber. There was sufficient light to make her way to the workbenches and beyond.

Strictly speaking, those who worked there needed no rest at all. But even they were granted a few hours of respite, Hephaestus in his bed chamber, his wife at rest in a bower redolent with herbs and roses, Venga's sisters propped, switched off, against the walls of a long corridor, an akimbo line of golden-skinned femininity.

In heaven, no one expected a thief.

Venga gathered her first clones, mortal ones on this trip, shrinking and bagging them in a pouch slung by her side and spiriting her booty past the stables again.

"Don't tell a soul," she said, her face so close to his that his breath tickled her cheeks.

"I won't," gruffed Gregor, admiration tinged with lust in his eyes.

"Good boy."

She blew him a kiss, held his gaze a moment more, rose up, and shot away toward the Tooth Fairy's island.

CHAPTER NINE
LOVE, LUST, AND
REPEATED FAILURES

Weeks passed.

Exhausted from hours of lovemaking, Rachel and Anya begged off another tumble, at least for a little while. A full moon draped its off-white light across their bodies.

"We need to catch our breath, darling," said Rachel.

"Of course, sweetheart. Finding it hard to keep up with your jolly old elf, eh?"

Anya went along. "You're a wonder, Claus."

Rachel loved him so.

Ever since he had fought with Pan on the plains of Tartarus and accepted the goat god as his alter ego, there was so much more of him to love and so much more intensity to his ardor.

Rough sex, frequent and impassioned—augmenting the tender lovemaking that had always been Santa's stock in trade—was one outcome. What was more, he seemed now inexhaustible, erect again in a matter of seconds, and overpoweringly joyous when he sank his perfect penis into them.

Rachel took advantage of the hiatus.

"Dear one," she said, "I'm concerned about the lack of progress in the psyche factory."

One eyebrow twitched. "It isn't going well?"

"I've been soft-pedaling my frustrations to Wendy. No need to worry her. But please think about stepping in yourself."

Santa laughed. "Really I can't—"

"I know it makes you queasy, coming into contact with grown-up mortals and their faults. But it's become clear that Fritz and the others have met their match. They're ill equipped for the kinds of problems they've been encountering."

"Such skilled craftsmen, ill equipped?" said Santa. "I'd have thought by now. . . ."

"Then there's Aphrodite."

"What about Aphrodite?"

"They can't keep their eyes off her. It's nothing she's doing to provoke them. But your dear helpers are such innocents. It's hard enough working out the intricacies of the human psyche—such a complex mechanism it is, the parts packed so tight together, the connecting tissue byzantine in its construction.

"Add in the Goddess of Love, whose least feint at a move captivates them.

"The unacknowledged satyr stirs inside them, their cocks rise, and they simply don't know what to make of it.

"One thing is clear: They're finding it impossible to concentrate on the job at hand."

Santa looked troubled.

"They need guidance I can't give them. Magic time has been stretched to the max. And Valentine's Day is less than a month off."

"I'll . . . I'll talk to them. Maybe that will help."

It wasn't what Rachel had hoped for. But at least she had broached the subject and received a commitment from him.

Santa skated off the subject and gave a loving leer. "I'm good for a few dozen more climaxes. How about you two lovely ladies?"

"Always," said Anya. "Have at us!"

Rachel concurred.

And Santa's magnificent passion rose once more. So generous he was, so full of delight and gratitude at his wives' loveliness, so flat-out hungry for them despite having kissed and caressed every micro-inch of their bodies millions of times before.

Rachel delighted in their bed, a doze-worthy, swive-worthy place, a place of love and comfort.

And Santa's prick since he had gotten cozy with Pan had no discernible down time.

Up and raring to go right away.

And go they went!

***

The following morning, the elves reconvened in the psyche factory, no closer to a solution than when they had begun.

Fritz had never felt such anguish.

Rachel was generous with her managerial guidance. But the engineering savvy had been left to him, Ludwig, and Herbert, and the task had gotten the best of them.

A disassembled clone of Frank Worthington's psyche lay before them. Hephaestus, his wife, and his golden girls were still asleep, unable to distract. Early morning had proven, such as it was, to be their most fruitful time.

Then in walked Rachel, Santa with her for a change, and their spirits lifted.

"Good morning, all," he said, taking the time to hug every one of them, some two hundred strong pressed against his warm rotundity.

"Now lads," continued Santa, "I understand from my lovely wife that things are at a standstill. Have I got that right?"

Murmurs from all sides, mingled with an eagerness for solution.

"What seems to be the problem?"

Fritz began to speak, but in chimed Ludwig, one cautious eye asquint.

"Damned thing's defeating us, I'd say. Not to insult the Creator, but we're not talking about a few design flaws here. The scale of this disaster is massive, Santa. Failure seems engineered into the thing. Could hardly have been planned worse. One crumble leads to ten more, and they likewise, like toppling dominoes.

"We've reconstituted our Mister Worthington's sad little psyche tens of thousands of times, examining its makeup, its construction, how the fool thing functions or fails to function. As soon as we arrive at a redesign for one tiny piece of the puzzle, everything else falls apart.

"At the dorm we're up all night, tossing snippets of conversation back and forth, ideas for improvements which in the feverishly fanciful light of the moon seem promising but which falter and fail at the workbench.

"It's the most damnable botch of an engineering job I've ever seen. Better to throw the whole thing out and start afresh. Not that that's about to happen."

Ludwig scowled at himself.

"Listen to me gas on, will you? No more excuses, no more bitching and moaning, no more gnashing of teeth from this elf. We'll get the motherfucker done, given time, patience, and the wherewithal to keep our panic down. We always have. Hold us to it, Santa, and we'll come through."

But these were clearly empty boasts and not one elf chimed in to support Ludwig's feeble attempt to rally their spirits.

Santa's distaste with adult mortals was palpable as he turned to Fritz's place at the workbench.

"Restore it, please."

Fritz's hands danced above the psyche. Instantly it took on wholeness again.

Santa leaned forward, tentative his hands as they hovered over the psyche.

His eyes drilled into it.

Then something changed in him. Something that seemed both trivial and monumental.

"No wonder they're the way they are."

He lifted off the over-psyche and peered into the basic foundation beneath.

"This is what mortals have to work with? Why, it's a wonder there are any saints at all."

Fritz held his breath. Would the master craftsman dig in at last, take over, turn his considerable skills to the daunting task?

Then Santa flinched.

"You boys have your work cut out for you, there's no question about it.

"My advice? Wear blinders. Not literally, though I wouldn't be opposed. Aphrodite and the gilded ones are beauties indeed. I understand that. They distract in the most enthralling way. But I beg you to save that for late night gabfests. If you don't figure out how to reverse engineer these psyches and soon, all

58

of this—our dear community as well—may vanish in a puff of might-have-been."

Santa glanced at them by turns.

"Fritz, Herbert, Ludwig, are you ready to renew your efforts, tackle it full force, eke out a solution by dint of brute strength if you have to?"

"We'll try, Santa," said Fritz, hoping his tepid words would draw the saint into the fray.

"Good lad. Good lads, all. Carry on then. I expect to hear wondrous news soon."

With that, he turned on his boot heel and left them to a new day of heartbreaks and disasters.

CHAPTER TEN
THE SQUATTING IMP AND A REPRIEVE FROM DEATH

Fritz and Ludwig again brought Frank Worthington to the North Pole.

They had asked Santa and Hephaestus for advice.

The blacksmith had been no help at all. "You'll get nowhere with that one," he had said with a laugh. "If you don't hone in on exactly the right changes to his psyche, he'll not be cooperative. Goddamn stubborn bastard isn't prone to self-examination. Give up on him, say I."

Santa, by contrast, listened most politely to their frustration. "Do your best, boys," he said. "The poor man was probably thrown by the sudden shift in his locale. Next time, bring him here more gently. And tell him why you brought him here. The sorry little fellow could use some orienting."

Though Santa had been the soul of patience, Fritz detected a rising level of anxiety in him.

The elves brought Worthington northward little by little this time, soothing him all the way until he stood before them in the psyche factory.

"Not you guys again. When do I get to meet the Big Cheese? Mister Ho-Ho-Ho? Don't I rate?"

Ludwig began, "We hadn't planned to—"

Fritz broke in. "Santa has entrusted you to us. You see, the human race is in quite a pickle." He filled the mortal in on the big picture and his role in supplying the catastrophe's tipping point.

"An argument with Krista, even a few harsh words, doesn't seem to merit such importance. Are you sure about this?"

They said they were.

And he, with hesitation, agreed to cooperate.

But alas, he was completely inarticulate and without the skill to observe and comment intelligently on his plight.

"Does this help?" Fritz would ask, making a tweak to the

man's psyche. "Do you feel any less inclined to yell at your wife?"

And Worthington would always say, "Who can tell? I think so. I can't be sure."

Finally, he lost patience with them. "Hey, aren't you guys supposed to be crack elves? Isn't tinkering your specialty? All I see are a couple of bumbling oafs. If the human race has to count on your expertise, we're royally fucked, far as I can tell. Why are you wasting my time?"

Then things got heated.

It was nothing Fritz and Ludwig said. No. Escalation came entirely from Worthington.

And once again, agonizing over what seemed an impossible task, they sent him back, mid-rant.

Ludwig shook his head. "Damned impossible!"

Moonlight splashed across Santa's bedroom.

Anya inhaled and exhaled in that way of hers that nearly turned into a snore but never did. Rachel lay beside her. So lovely, both of them.

Santa slipped out of bed, slid back his closet door, and suited up.

His office? Not this time.

Such peace lay open to him as he made his way across the commons, his helpers abed in their dorm, only Gregor standing distant at the stable door, arms folded, judging, always judging.

Santa passed through the entrance to the psyche factory, the vast work area dimly lit by backlighting. Nobody in sight. He could tell he was in heaven, all around him a comfort he hadn't earned.

At the elves' workbench, he surveyed the scattered psyches in various states of disarray.

How could one heal such wounds?

What tools to use? These things seemed to respond to intricate, delicate suggestion. But was that the only approach? In the morning, he would bring in Fritz, see if Helmut the clockmaker might be assigned the task of developing probes and ratchets, calipers and clips, hand tools or mechanized marvels never before seen, sufficiently machined and oiled to tweak the innards of these beasties with success.

A golden girl slipped in, gave him a spare nod, and floated up into the back areas. He had seen this one before. A beguiling temptress, were she made of flesh and bone. Hmmm, she was a temptress even in gold. The beauteous rise of her breasts seemed larger than before, the easy oil in her walk as buttocks and groin swept along like streams of gold.

Despair surged in to overlay Santa's lust.

What a fraud I am, he thought, with my pep talks.

It's clear what Fritz and the others want from me. There's no way I'll sully my hands with these things, no matter how understandable the fallen state of mortal man is. Out will pop Pan, putting his peculiar stamp on whatever fixes I make. He'll fly in under the radar. No telling what impact he might have.

Then there was the manufacture of toys, falling way behind.

The elves working here were virtually useless, their time eaten up in frustration and failure, their esteem crushed.

And Valentine's Day was drawing ever nearer.

Rage rose in him, pointless and impotent.

Surrender to your helplessness, he thought. Throw yourself on God's mercy. How much nearer than here could the Father be?

Santa fell to his knees, bowed his head, and clasped his hands. "Dear Father," he prayed, "our forces are overtaxed. We've stretched magic time to the limit. Even with that stretching, our toy making falters and our work on the human psyche goes nowhere.

"Grant me more helpers, I beg of You. More elves. New ones if need be. All of my former satyrs, I know, are accounted for in my contingent of helpers. But a doubled or—dare I ask it?—a trebled staff might give us a fighting chance.

"Let me not presume to suggest solutions. Thy will be done, always.

"This I pray in the name of Your Son, begging for succor in our time of greatest need.

"Amen."

***

Santa returned to his bedroom, undressed, and slipped into a dejected sleep. High up against the ceiling, Gronk hovered invisible, wholly undetected.

There was something damnably exciting about the thought of squatting on Santa's torso, inhaling the rich tobacco aromas in his huge white fluff of a beard, and oozing oily suggestions into his tufted ears.

All while two nightgowned goddesses lay close by, their scents beguiling Gronk's nostrils, scents of fresh-baked bread, of ivy and holly berries, of their birth slits so recently swollen and filled—slits like Mommy's slit only on nicer females who would never tear him apart the way she did.

Gronk was eternally erect as usual. There were no inappropriate places, none, for the thick tower of his fuckstalk to rise up.

So he leapt lightly onto the snoring elf and let his engorgement thwap at that fat belly. Santa's snore suspended an instant, but his sleep's depth lessened not one iota.

"O wise one," said Gronk, "you're so right to steer clear of mortal psyches. One of your helpers can find his way to a solution without your intervention."

A smile played about Santa's lips.

"Look at it this way. Fritz and the others have no inkling of their pasts as satyrs. They are incapable of sullying these psyches. You on the other hand rightly hold back, mistrusting Pan's hand.

"Besides, think of the children. They deserve, the nice ones anyway, the finest of toys. They deserve a Santa unspoiled. Pour your sweet and tender energies into preparations for Christmas. Do you really believe the human race has a tipping point? Isn't it possible that Wendy has simply projected her worst fears and not shown reality at all?

"She's a dear girl, that Wendy.

"Still, you're in charge. Let the work proceed, if proceed it must. But what's the rush? There is no rush. Not really. All deliberate speed and nothing speedier.

"The North Pole has a certain integrity about it, a certain peace. Don't jeopardize those qualities. Rush not into the thoughtless disintegration of all you've fashioned here over the centuries."

It was never easy to see how effective his words were in not merely penetrating the sleeping mind, but in sticking there and sprouting, the roots thrust so deep that the waking mind would take one path over another.

But the work had begun, Gronk thought.

Night after night, he would be at the fat and jolly bastard, digging in, digging at his mind like a prisoner spooning his way through a stone wall.

Dawn lay hours ahead. No need to rush.

It was a lovely bedroom, lovely surroundings, lovely aromas, the loveliest of immortal squeezes close by.

Persistence paid off, they said.

Gronk would see about that.

As the Father God suffered the impudent assault of Santa's prayer, a wicked smile played upon His lips.

"Why," asked the Shame Son, "do you pay that fatty any mind at all? He's always whining about something not quite right with Your creation."

God looked vacantly at the scrawny creature seated on His lap. "Usually I don't. It's different this time. One moment. There, that should do the trick."

Now as you might suspect—astute reader that you are—in the microsecond between *moment* and *there*, the Father had gone off elsewhere, done elsewhat to elsewhom, and returned without so much as a hint of disappearance. He was that good.

Allow me to elaborate.

The Father manifested upon the plains where ages ago, deZeussified and become the God of Wrath, he had slaughtered thousands of wood nymphs and their goatish, prick-engorged satyrs, many of them paired up, erotically entwined, and creamed with copulation even in that final panic-laden moment.

Spared only—in that instant of bloodletting upon a gore-soaked plain—were Pan-turned-to-Santa; all the satyrs, now become elves; the pine nymph Pitys, Pan's favorite whom Saint Nick took as his wife Anya; and the ash nymph Adrasteia, cutting a deal to spare her life by agreeing to become the Tooth Fairy.

How bad could that be? Adrasteia had wondered, and soon found out.

Now, upon this wooded land thick with pine, ash, and poplar, reaching back heavenward into His psyche factory's archives where the souls of the dead were kept, the Father pulled forth the psyches of a sufficient number of wood nymphs to match precisely the number of Santa's elves, and restored their bodies as they had been before He had wasted them.

Into them He breathed the breath of life.

From them came shouts of release from death.

Atlanteia and Phoebe lay near one another, asprawl and panting, where they had felt the blow that stilled them forever.

Chrysopeleia of the double cunt stood planted firm, legs apart, dripping the fluid of lust upon the earth, as defiant now as when death's blow had felled her.

Dryope, Erato, Phigalia, Tithorea, arm in arm in arm in arm, hugged one another with hungry ferocity and gazed about at their disoriented sisters.

There too stood Aegle, Eritheia, and Hesperia—the daughters of Hesperos, God of the Evening Star—who had once guarded the Tree of the Golden Apples.

"Listen up," boomed the Father. "Savor your final lungsful of nymphic air. Savor the wild, untamed, and untamable passions coursing through your veins. For I have restored you to life for a new purpose.

"You I shall turn to elves, fetching female ones, your lives among these trees forgotten, your memory of drunken debaucheries wiped clean. Silence I shall take as assent, and you have one more breath in which to object, if object you choose—though that breath shall be your last.

"No objections? Good."

The Father swept a hand toward them.

Gone at once the scents of sexual excess, gone the lusty thighs and breasts, gone the ivy windings about arms and legs, the crushed-berry, come-on colorings of daubed lips and labia, the tresses wild and savagely grippable, the mad and maddening eyes that seconds before had flared with desire unquenchable.

There they stood, a new kind of sisterhood in green garb that matched the outfits worn by Fritz, Gregor, Herbert, and the whole ridiculous crew at the North Pole. The cuteness they gave off counterparted the male cuteness of those they would soon join.

Blank slates for an instant they stood.

Then the Father stuffed their heads with false memories, as he had done ages ago for Pan and his satyrs.

Stories danced in their eyes, stories that made glorious sense and filled their countenances with delight. They giggled and swooned together, exchanging excited words.

Hushed in wonder, they turned to Him.

But before they could speak, He gestured them gone, dotting the woods about the North Pole with small huts, each housing one of His new creations.

"That should do it," said the Father, deeply self-satisfied as usual. "An answer to Santa's prayer."

Back He swept to His exalted throne, but that's where you good people came in.

Scene over!

CHAPTER ELEVEN
DISENGAGED,
REVOLUTION, ENGAGED

Snatched from the depths of dream, the elves woke to a thunderous crack that came in from all directions and pinned them to their beds.

Ordinarily, such a blast would have thrust fear deep inside them, so abruptly did it shatter the peace of the breaking dawn.

But this joyful noise came wrapped in amazement, a gift descended from heaven, a wondrous thing shortly to be visited upon them.

Out of their nightshirts they tumbled, scrambling with haste into pants, jerkins, slippers, and belled caps.

Heinrich's six bodies were the first to squeeze through the door into the commons, followed by a bright green outpouring of helpers, as elf after elf shot into the growing dawn.

"Over there," said Fritz.

"And there," echoed Herbert.

Several others pointed excitedly to the green-garbed figures emerging from the woods.

"Well, well. What have we here?" boomed Santa, as he and his wives appeared on the porch. "Come forth, you marvelous creatures. Don't be shy."

Laughter sparkled in his voice, a sound all too rare these days.

"Look, Daddy," said Wendy. "Female elves!" She raced across the commons to the nearest one, threw her arms around her, took her hand, and brought her forward.

The other females followed from all sides.

"Welcome to you all," said Santa as they clustered around him. "I prayed for reinforcements. And what reinforcements the Almighty has sent!"

To the one arm-in-arm with Wendy: "What's your name, pretty one?"

"Gretchen," she fluted. "I paint miniatures and dab color onto porcelain figurines. But I can fill in where I'm needed. We all can."

"And you, dear?"

"I'm Hildegard," said the redhead on Gretchen's left. "My specialty is constructing kits for large pretend kiddie trucks and cars."

Santa laughed. "'Tis a wise elf that knows what she's best at. Heaven forbid a mismatch!"

The blonde behind Wendy wildly waved her hand, exclaiming, "I can do anything and I can do it well. But the thing I love most is turning out every last piece of a board game, awash with bright colors. You may call me Sieglinde, Santa, sir, 'cause that's my name."

"And so I shall, sweet Sieglinde."

Thus Santa brought each of their number into the community, giving her a fatherly hug, and declaring the rest of the day a holiday, given over to celebration and thanks to the Almighty.

"Tomorrow with gusto and urgency shall we resume our efforts in workshop and psyche factory. But today we feast. Today we welcome these capable new elves to our midst, new members of our close-knit family. Let the festivities begin!"

And begin they did.

Gregor, wrapped in bafflement and puzzled beyond belief, harrumphed from his stable door as usual. But the others threw themselves into holiday mode, brief though it would be.

Quint and Gronk, hovering unnoticed, took it all in and zoomed off to report this startling development to Venga and the Tooth Fairy.

CHAPTER TWELVE
MEMBRUM VIRILE
PRAEPUTIO RETRACTO

The following morning, after Santa's brief workshop pep talk, the new arrivals went straight to work.

He marveled at how well they melded, smoothly scattered in among the others, fresh new stools and workbenches somehow not overcrowding the work space.

Particularly delightful—Wendy remarked on this during their evening walk in the woods—were the male elves' looks of awe and amazement.

Funny though how an erection of the wrong sort can cast a new light on things. At two fifty-four a.m. that night, Saint Nicholas sprang—and spring was indeed the operative word—awake.

One moment, enfolded in dreamland adventures.

The next, without warning or transition, eye-wide above, blood-thick below.

This wasn't the generous, other-directed boner he loved to sink into Anya and Rachel's honey drippers. No, this accursed hard-on throbbed and thundered, insisted and provoked, roused roaring hot lust in his brain, set a-boiling a raging need to find new quim—or better still, quim he had fingered and fucked in his long forgotten past.

No matrimonially sanctioned cunt would do. Only this would satisfy—the sweat and gush of some new vaginal clutch, gripping tight his urgent flesh.

More disturbing still: The womanly images that fed his desires came straight from the workshop, in skirts and long tresses.

Their façades were so innocent. But behind them, he caught glimpses of the lubricious creatures they had once been. For these were not new but recycled creations from the Father's storehouse of goodies.

69

These were wood nymphs.

Resurrected sisters of the Tooth Fairy.

And Pan's former woodland fuckmates.

Santa hadn't prayed to God for female elves. He had most especially not prayed for once lascivious beings whose buried pasts must, most assuredly, rise up to try the innocence of his helpers and himself.

The taunting reminders in the merest turn of the head, in a brief glance, in the subtle purse of the lips, even in the occasional gape-mouthed yawn—these would not only hint at their past lives as tree nymphs and the nymphomania at the heart of those lives. They would also serve to highlight and bring into recall the satyric features of the males working side by side with them.

Anya, herself a former pine nymph, had given no hint that she noticed anything amiss.

But in the moonlight splashed across their bed, and with the needy erection that brought Pan's hormones to the fore, all uncertainty fled from Santa's mind.

He was tempted to stroke his wives awake for a late night tumble—not an unusual occurrence—but in his current state of other-directed lust, that would feel wrong. Instead, he allowed memories of ancient days to surge in and feed his desires.

Back then, in a continual state of drunkenness and fleshly debauch as the King of the Satyrs (not that Pan, a commanding presence indeed, gave the ghost of a fuck for titles or power), he had reveled in a swiftly rotating whirligig of lovers, his cock always up, never without female lubricant, eternally slick for the next penetrate-and-piston.

Through the woods on thunderous hooves, joyous and playful pursuits were his. The grab, the grasp, the insertion of rough-furred fingers. Shoving her against an oak—no idea her name, no need to waste time on questions of identity— pounding the daylights out of her.

Still they were vivid and unique to him, but by scent and sense, not by the prisons of words.

Had he been blind, the smell and taste of them, the skin

70

tones englowed, their squeals and deep-throated gasps before he plugged their body-holes with his hot sex—these at once identified them.

All the while, Santa stroked himself.

And now, soundlessly crying from part of his psyche, soundlessly reveling from the rest, he spent his spirit in a waste of shame.

Pure Pan came to the fore.

Stress had been Santa's constant companion.

But this new complication made it worse.

It boded ill indeed, the subtle reminders of their pagan pasts, his deep aversion to grown-up mortals, and the spillover into his feelings for nice kids.

Now Santa lay there—clammy his belly, drenched his nightshirt—and wept silent tears.

The fifteenth of January, Rachel, Wendy, and Fritz showed up unannounced at Santa's office.

He was poised to launch into an effusive greeting. Then, seeing their faces, he said, "Please come in."

Fritz closed the door behind them.

"Sweetheart," said Rachel, "we'll come straight to the point. Fritz and his fellow workers have explored every avenue. They're no closer to a fix for the human psyche than when they began."

"I'm afraid that's so, Santa," said Fritz, dole and sorrow filling his eyes.

"Now it's true," continued Rachel, "that they've been able to patch up several of Frank Worthington's failures, tweaks to his battered over-psyche. But without changes to the under-psyche, those patches shred to nothing. And the under-psyche has defied every attempt at change, every tool Fritz and the others invent to probe and tinker with the bad spots. Everything falls to pieces. They have to start over."

Fear gripped Santa and great reluctance. "You'd like me to step in."

"Yes, Daddy," said Wendy, doing what she could to mute her anguish. "It's the only way."

Santa hung fire. He looked at each of his visitors in turn. Then he went to his roll top desk and took out a thick stack of papers from one drawer.

"You see these? It's a list I once made of everything that's wrong with grown-up human beings. I was as comprehensive as I could manage before I had to turn away in disgust. Here, Wendy, take a look. Tell me if this is fixable."

Wendy took the list, heavy in her hands.

As she read it, despair seized her, but it was soon replaced by defiance.

"Piece of cake," she said. "Yes, all of this can be fixed. But only by you, Father. Our hopes and the hopes of humankind rest with you."

"Well."

He paused for a very long time. His breath moved with surprising freedom. He looked at each of them with the purest love.

"We can't let the human race slip down the rabbit hole, now can we? It seems I can't keep them at arm's length any longer. Let me be honest. I harbor certain fears about getting my hands dirty in the muck and mire of their unworthy ways. Above all I fear that my deep love for good little boys and girls may turn to distaste, even loathing. But to do nothing will lead, surely, to the end of Christmas as we know it, will it not?"

"I'm afraid so, Santa," said Fritz. "Please, sir. We can't let that happen."

"You're right. We can't. There are times when one must lean into fear, acknowledge it, honor it, and dig into its bitter feast. Such a time has now arrived."

The four of them shared an embrace, Santa drawing on their strength to shore up his courage.

Then he went straight to the psyche factory.

At his arrival, the embattled elves greeted him with special warmth. Pinning their hopes on him? Well, why not? It was make or break time, and break was not an option.

Santa stole a glance at Aphrodite, who as usual ignored

him as she helped her husband and his crew of golden girls process newborn psyches. Such was her beauty that she had no need to shoot come-hither looks in anyone's direction. One such look would have stopped his ancient heart.

"All right, lads," he said, "give jolly old Saint Nick plenty of breathing room. Fritz, Herbert, Ludwig, and anyone who'd care to chime in, fill me in on what you've learned about this man's under-psyche and every failed fix you've attempted. No need to reinvent the wheel."

With gusto and animation, the three project leads launched into their tale of woe.

Santa tracked every detail, pressing it like seed corn into his fertile mind. Despite the urgency of what he was about, his thoughts strayed continually to the female elves now hard at work here, to Hephaestus's golden helpers, and to the unbounded beauty of the Goddess of Love. How obsessed he had become with the female form, how charged his erotic imaginings.

From his elves' reaction, they clearly detected the shift in him, though a thick overlay of innocence kept them from understanding it.

The newly arrived females shifted and swayed one or two micro-inches from their once lascivious selves. Their former identities were obvious to him, even to the point of names.

Where Fritz and the others saw Kirsten, Heidi, and Ursula, they lived vividly in Santa's memory as Acantha of the high sweet cry, Chrysopeleia in all her insatiable hunger, and Dryope against an oak, its bark dimpling her back, his prick high up inside her and thrusting to meet her lust.

His male helpers were clearly much enamored of them, in the way a ga-ga schoolboy might carry the books of a breast-budding young thing through the corridors of middle school.

At first glance, they seemed a minor distraction to his lads. On closer inspection, the cumulative effects were evident. What God had meant as an aid to their toy making instead further hindered their efforts.

Still, though the females answered his subtle winks and nods with innocent flirtation, Santa felt no real temptation to stray from his marriage vows—not, at least, with them.

Nor with the golden girls, as cool and lovely their auric beauty, as curious as he was about the taste of a gilded nipple or the oily clutch of a golden cunt about his cock. Well, all right, perhaps she who had nodded to him, the sway of whose hips came often to his mind.

But Aphrodite was a different story.

She needed no special moves to move him.

One glimpse of the goddess seared Santa's brain, setting off the wildest of fantasies.

With all of his being, his generosity included, he craved an affair with her.

Ridiculous!

He dearly loved Rachel and Anya, the depth of their connection as deep as could be—in constant growth, each point of commonality thriving and growing as their time together ticked by.

And my God, the lovemaking they shared. It was the ultimate in spontaneous, time-banishing play, a wild exuberant foray into toys, masks, and costumes, into coconut oil freely slathered, into full-tilt voyeurism as he lay back and watched them enjoy their Sapphic dance of pleasure.

A side trip into the wonderland of Aphrodite would surely be detrimental—a secret side trip at that—to his marriage. He dare not confess his lusts to Rachel and Anya, not even idly, lest they fear they were no longer enough for him.

Wait, where am I?

Ah, yes, sitting with Frank Worthington's stubborn under-psyche, the Goddess of Love standing not fifty feet away, Fritz and the other elves pregnant with expectation.

Old reliable Santa would figure it all out for them.

There he sat, not the ghost of an idea coming to him, and tasted the beginnings of the frustration that had plagued his helpers for weeks.

"Quite a tough nut to crack, this," he joked.

No one laughed.

CHAPTER THIRTEEN
IMMORTAL MISCHIEF AND A
SMITH'S TUTORIAL

Five days went by.

Far into the evening, Gregor sat all a-glower in his office chair, his desk spotless except for a legal pad on the blotter, nested in the green glare of lantern light.

List upon list lay before him, penned with great fury and precision in an immaculate script.

What he planned to do when he took over.

How he would whip the elves into shape.

Dozens of ideas for the redesign and refurbishing of the big house, once Santa had been booted out.

Punishments he would visit upon naughty boys and girls. Severely scaled-back toy deliveries to the ones that only put on a convincing act of being nice.

Why reward what was expected?

A Spartan scaling back of meals for the work force at the North Pole. Cancelling their day of frolic after the Christmas Eve deliveries. Far more regimen. Far less tolerance of eccentricities. By God, they'd learn to be more like him or out they'd go with the trash!

Gregor harrumphed at his lists.

"Sheer nonsense."

Idle scribblings, all of it, never to be enacted. Just a goddamned pipe dream, this future usurpation.

Gregor made to throw down his quill pen.

He stopped himself, the thought of ink flung in odd directions, a random mess, making him shudder.

Just then, a vision of loveliness gleaming gold in the moonlight appeared at the stable door.

"By the way," she continued, as though no time had passed since her first appearance, "Venga's my name. You're Gregor. I'm your intended. You're mine. Now that that's settled, I'm coming in."

And in she came.

He was appalled and thrilled at her audacity.

She came boldly up to him and lifted the legal pad, flipping through its pages.

"Big plans, bold and ballsy. I like that." She dropped it onto the desk top. "So what's the hold up?"

"I dream big dreams." He hated himself for leveling with her. It felt weak. But the pain of her beauty hurt his eyes and pried things out of him. "When it comes to acting on them, I haven't a clue."

She laughed.

Anyone else's laugh would have wounded.

Venga's laugh thrilled.

"Here's what you'll do. Tomorrow morning, crack of dawn, you'll track Saint Nick to his lair, shut the door, collar him, and issue your demands."

"But there's no way I could—"

"Listen carefully. If you don't do as I say, I'll walk out that door and never return. Otherwise, I'll come back. You'll see a whole lot more of me." She leaned closer, the golden gleam of her breasts raising beads of sweat on his brow, her honeycomb scent tormenting his nose.

"Except, of course, when I blindfold you."

He faltered. "You've got a lot of nerve."

Venga smiled. "And you just got lucky."

The next morning, Santa faked a cheery hello to his elves in the workshop, then ensconced himself in his office, poring over engineering diagrams and graph paper thick with pencil scrawls, cross outs, and sudden inspirations that went nowhere or doubled back upon themselves.

A sharp rap on the door startled him.

Rising, he put his best face on. When he opened the door and saw which elf stood there, his delight turned genuine. "Come in, dear friend Gregor, and welcome to you. It's good to see you out and about, you keep so much to the stables these days.

"Wonderful care, by the way, of my team. In tiptop shape

as always for the Christmas deliveries.

"Please take a seat."

Gregor's sour expression hadn't changed. But then it never did.

Ice in his voice: "I prefer to stand."

At this, Santa broke into a hearty, belly-shaking laugh. "Well then, I honor your preference. Forgive me if I sit, won't you?"

And sit he did, his hands idly brushing the papers before him so that two or three leafed lazily to the floor. He bent and rustled them up, sighing at them.

"Thorny problem, this psyche business."

Gregor crossed his arms with renewed resolve and raised one eyebrow in a bushy caret. "You are to step down. I'll take over."

Santa smiled and waved a hand. "Often are the times I would like nothing better. This may well be one of them."

"I want your clothing," Gregor forged ahead. "Your sleigh too. Your house. This office. Everything that's yours."

Santa stopped smiling.

"Be serious, Gregor. I know how upset you were with your fellow elves over that nosepicking business, the photos of you, projected on the bed sheet in the Chapel, digging edible boogers out of Comet and Cupid's nostrils. But really, this is too much. I'm not about to—"

'I'll have your wives and your daughter too. You can feed and groom the reindeer. It carries such an easy burden of responsibility."

Santa felt his face redden. Pan began to bubble and brew inside him. Had his stress been so transparent as to earn him the disrespect of one of his finest elves?

"See here, little fellow." He shook his finger in the upstart's face. "You are way out of line. You need to march back out that door, reseat your head properly on your shoulders, and return with a respectful knock and a civil tongue."

Gregor flapped his jaws but nothing came out.

It was as if he expected capitulation and when it wasn't forthcoming, his script had run dry.

"Harrumph," he said with halting determination. And again, "Harrumph."

Then he marched out that door, all right.

But return he did not.

Venga despised the island's dreariness, its continual overcast, gloom, and rain, and the frigidly cold Quint and his twelve loathsome siblings.

The living conditions were, of course, several cuts above Tartarus and Venga's enforced concubinage with the God of the Underworld. The close, killing confinement of that place and her captor's hellish stench made the Tooth Fairy's island a paradise by comparison.

Still, said fairy was a crude piece of work.

Good for a quick volley of over-the-top orgasms in the rough and tumble of bloodletting sex.

But that had quickly paled, especially after her first glimpse of the North Pole and the malleable Gregor. There was sufficient steel in his backbone to topple, with her help, Santa Claus but not enough to best her in erotic combat or in any other spats, squabbles, and knock-down-drag-out's their future might hold.

Now, on the twenty-fourth of January, she surveyed the purloined psyches she had cloned and smuggled out of the psyche factory—mortal ones on her left, immortal on her right.

Because Santa Claus was nowhere near a solution to his engineering nightmare, Venga found herself at a loss when it came to countering or undermining his moves.

Still, reports from Gronk and Quint, as well as her examination of Santa's elves' failed experiments, gave her practice. That would hold her in good stead if ever the jolly old fuck achieved a breakthrough or finally made up his goddamned mind.

His efforts to create tools were laughable.

Unlike the North Polar crew, Venga had had the immeasurable advantage of watching Hephaestus at work for centuries. She had never focused on slavishly handing off over-psyches or receiving full psyches, but on the skilled dance of the god's hands spidering over each of his constructions, the brilliant bent of his mind that shone in his eyes, the deft body movements at his command despite his broken limbs.

Those memories she had turned to good use in her experiments here on the island.

Easily countered and undone, the elfin tweaks.

It was a simple matter—and surely likely always to escape detection—to try one or two changes on stolen psyches, observe the mortal before and after they had been instituted, then withdraw them. If some of her subjects wound up in loony bins, and quite a few did, well, that was just the luck of the draw and nothing she need concern herself about.

Only God Himself or some observant angel was ever likely to tie her to these earthly mishaps.

Undetectable damage.

That would be her eventual goal.

All she needed were tweaks laid atop Santa's fixes with such delicacy that he would never see the doom before it befell, ready to spring forth and negate his infernal meddlings, swiftly inflicted with no hope of countering them.

Once Saint High and Mighty had failed in so public and decisive a way, he would retire—or be retired—in shame. In his wake, she and Gregor would sail.

And a new era would begin.

The Tooth Fairy swooped in to disrupt her musings, Quint and Gronk following behind.

"Well?" Defiance. "Anything?"

"My answer is the same as the last hundred times: When and if Santa Claus perfects his ultimate gift to the human race, we'll have our Trojan Horse and I'll be able to pack it with proper Greeks."

"Stop calling him that."

"Pan, then. All right?"

Despite Adrasteia's obsession with Venga's efforts, the golden girl could sniff the radiant lust for Quint rising from her skin. Mommy craved sonny boy's body, that oily, ice-cold brute so skilled at faking a brand of urbanity. Disgusting, but what could one expect of an ash nymph?

"Pan," she repeated. "Pan, the goat god we all love to hate. Satisfied?"

The Tooth Fairy glared at the cloned psyche in front of Venga. "Must have it."

"Are you listening?"

"Must."

"Sure, sure, okay. Just let me work in peace."

That didn't sit well with Adrasteia. An attack seemed imminent. With the Tooth Fairy, an attack *always* seemed imminent.

Truth was, Venga welcomed her attacks.

Their interactions in such moments always turned savage and sexual, swirling up in the air, their bodies mutually ravaged, their flesh torn, bones broken and reknitted, wounds opened and closing, blood, sweat, and sex fluids flowing profusely, spattering the sand below them with spent needs and needs that required new spending.

This time, however, Adrasteia, flinging a last lustful look at her youngest son and spitting back the word, "Must," swept up and away, her necklace of bloody teeth slapping at her chest like the clatter of tossed dice.

The golden hair at the back of Venga's neck, as thin and bunched as crushed wire, tingled as if by static.

Such sweet, savage love.

Maybe this island wasn't so bad after all.

Three days passed fruitlessly.

With less than a week remaining in January, Saint Nicholas, his stress level exceptionally high, talked Hephaestus into a private tutoring session.

Ushered out were the golden girls, Santa's helpers, Wendy, Rachel, and dear, sweet, darling Aphrodite.

Unnoticed as usual were Quint and Gronk, flies on the wall.

"Won't do you a lick of good. But God knows I'm willing," said Hephaestus.

"Yes, yes, of course," said Santa. "I just want a few tips on how to handle these psyches, a pointer or two about technique."

"You got it."

"I'd also value your thoughts on how the corruption sets in as mortals grow from infancy to adulthood, by what manner of means that happens."

The blacksmith laughed and shook his head. "I have no thoughts about such matters, valuable or not. Not in my charter.

"My job is to churn 'em out, create the fingerprint, hand 'em off, and go on to the next. If they're fated to screw up, squander their talents, or go whole-hog in some nasty direction and take lots of folks down with them, that's someone else's lookout, not mine."

Santa paled. "If you'll excuse my saying so, that's not very—"

"Charity ain't in my charter either. Haven't got the time for it. Haven't got the time for much of anything, this bunch breeds so fast and furious. Each wee fucker needs its precious little soul just right when it pops out of pouch and purse. Nearly half a million newborns a day on this godforsaken planet, not to mention the quarter million that die each day whose psyches need to be retired or recycled. I've scarcely got the time for this interview, if you'll pardon my saying so."

"I much prize your sacrifice and whatever you have to offer along these lines."

"Nothing a-tall is what I have to offer. Let's just stay on topic, shall we?"

Santa obsequiously agreed to that.

As if having freshly signed a pact, the ink still wet on its pages, Hephaestus launched into a twenty-minute monologue, stuffed to the gills with invaluable tips and tricks concerning the care and handling of the human psyche.

"And may I conclude," said he, "with this heartfelt sentiment, immortal to immortal: I don't envy you the task of fixing Zeus's fucked-up creation, nope, not one bit, not one iota, not one jot or tittle. I've squinted out at them and they are fucked six ways from Sunday, if you'll pardon my Anglo-Saxon. But better you than me trying to fix them, Mister Saint Nicholas, sir. Better by a long shot.

"Good luck dodging bullets, o courageous one. If anyone could do with some luck, it's you."

He swiveled about on his tall stool and stuck his index fingers in his mouth, ready to let out a whistle for his golden handmaidens.

"One thing more," said Santa.

Hephaestus swiveled back, glanced sharply at the huge chronometer that towered over his work, and said, "Out with it, man."

"Your time is precious," said Santa. "Mine too. So to the point: You are married to the loveliest, sexiest, most beautiful female in the world."

"Yes, yes, I know."

"Don't you ever get jealous? My elves steal glances at her. So, I must confess, do I."

"Of course you do. Every living creature with blood, breath, eyes, hormones, and half a heartbeat—male or female—goes crazy over Aphrodite.

"See here: I've got no time for jealousy. It doesn't serve me well. She's the Goddess of Love, for Christ's sake. What do you expect? I was ridiculed once for giving a shit about such things, some crap with a net or something, all the Olympian gods laughing at me.

"I got no more shits to give in that department.

"I'm Aphrodite's anchor. She knows it. She'll never leave me, not for all eternity. That has to suffice. I get to sleep beside her. Why, sometimes, she even lets me touch her—and I mean thoroughly touch her, inside and out. Can you imagine what a privilege that is?"

"I'm pretty sure I can."

"Trust me, you can't."

Santa forged ahead. "She fires such thoughts in my mind, I—"

"You want to bed down with her, right? Swive my wife, skewer the fuck out or her, take her in whatever way your demanding little prick desires? Well, that'd be okay by me. I wouldn't care. I've got bigger fish to fry, what with this job and all. Truth is, I'd find it kinda flattering."

Santa abruptly lost the ability to breathe.

"Besides which, Aphrodite told me, quite recently in fact, that she finds you very attractive, what with your boundless generosity in this saintly incarnation and your legendary sexual prowess as Pan. She told me she wouldn't mind leaping your bones if only once, just to see if legend speaks true or is full of shit. Well, those weren't quite her words, but almost."

Santa opened his lips, then realized he had no idea what to say.

"Speechless? Naturally. Are we finished?"

"Oh there's just one more—"

"Sure, sure, there's always one more thing. Out with it, man. Chop-chop. Quick like a bunny."

"How did you and your wife get to keep your, you know, original identities? The rout of immortals and their death or transformation seemed pretty universal, way back when. Me, for example. The satyrs and the wood nymphs, Dionysus, Hermes, Zeus himself."

"I'll tell you how." The question had stirred up some fierce memory in the smith, resentment still burning after centuries. "I took that blowhard, that so-called king of the gods, behind the woodshed and gave him the tongue-lashing of his life. See here, I told him, the throne you plant your fat butt on, all the thrones on Mount Olympus, I created. Nobody else. Your armor, your sandals, your thunderbolts, everything you use, pick up, throw, give as gifts, eat your food from, your chariots, your combs, your clippers, your adornments, your divine shitter? Guess who made 'em. That's right. Hephaestus. And he what made 'em can unmake 'em. So you'd best leave me the fuck alone about this new identity bullshit. Leave my wife alone too. 'Cause I can fuck up your surroundings real right royally. And don't think I won't!"

He turned to Santa. "Nuff said?"

"Yes indeed."

"Good. Now let's get the others back in here and restart this infernal mechanism.

"Can't keep those newborns waiting!"

CHAPTER FOURTEEN
SANTA STEPS UP,
NEARLY STEPS BACK

Having thoroughly scrutinized under Hephaestus's tutelage the workings of the under-psyche and with a near photographic memory, Santa shut himself in his workshop office and toiled feverishly over a redraft of his blueprints, sensing he was on the right track at last.

The following morning, after an abbreviated walk to the Chapel with Wendy and a heartfelt prayer to the Father God for strength and success, he made straight for the psyche factory.

Santa gave his customary nod to Aphrodite and her husband, then turned to his elves.

"Lads," he said, "I need full focus at this workbench, no distractions, nothing that doesn't pertain to what I'm doing here. I'll be calling for a number of psyches from the archives, in various stages of development. It'll be your job to work out the most efficient means of delivering them."

Fritz and Herbert scrambled to put together a plan, recruiting, with Hephaestus's permission, half a dozen golden girls to assist.

Santa thought he recognized one of them from that night long ago. But her breasts were not exceptionally large today, nor her walk as lubricious as he recalled.

Then he set to work with a vengeance.

First he compared the starting points of several psyches at birth, tracing, through each mortal's life and development, how it happened that certain identifiable weaknesses in the foundational under-psyche reinforced—indeed, encouraged—deviant channels of thought, word, and deed in the over-psyche.

These, buttressed by corrupting tendencies in the surrounding society, in the echo chambers of ingrown clans, or in a family of intertwined psyches—each in some way morally or otherwise compromised—led a once innocent mortal down the garden path.

Naughty tendencies already nascent, or rooted and growing, were thus reinforced and exacerbated. And fresh tendencies toward naughtiness started to form.

Next, he had to identify as precisely as he could the botched places in the under-psyche that fed into each generalizable human failing.

And systematically, Fritz scribbling feverish notes by his side, Santa did just that.

Wendy dropped by as he began an examination of three particular psyches. She projected their futures as he looked over their present lives, shifting his focus between those glimpses and their psyches.

The first mortals Santa examined were Jacques and Dominique LaFramboise from Colmar, France.

After ten years of a neglected marriage spiraling out of control, they were flat out bored with one another. Jacques had a mistress, Dominique a lover. They limped along on inertia, though their daughter Marie had flown the nest long ago. Once the tipping point occurred, their boredom was fated to flare up, leading to verbal and physical fights, her near-death from choking, and his sad descent into sullen anger. Even so, they would choose to stay together.

Santa was appalled. They were miserable now and that misery was destined to intensify, trapping them further in a mutual death grip.

He noted the failings in their psyches, feeling light in the head as the confounded nature of those failings hit home.

Next he turned to Willard Frist, a fifty-two-year-old man on his way to a massive stroke. Though the CEO of a company in Akron, Ohio that made educational toys, Frist hated kids, shamed his employees, loved his bean counters, loved a sales force that overpromised, and drove like slaves the workers on his assembly line as well as his toy designers. In the future, he would be far worse. A disgruntled employee would one day go postal on his colleagues. But Frist would whip out a pistol and off the guy, then in a mad frenzy open fire himself on his goggle-eyed, do-nothing workforce.

"Ouch," said Santa, his face turning white. Such an ugly set of engrained patterns in Frist's psyche.

Finally, he turned to Gillian Barnes, a rich heiress throwing her life away on trinkets, junkets, and jet set frivolity. Gillian lived in a posh London penthouse, fancying herself the superior of anyone who dared cross her path. When the world tumbled into wrack and ruin, she would dip further into drink and drugs, go into increasingly dicey parts of the city looking for exotic sexual practices, and one day vanish without a trace.

"How sad," said Wendy.

Santa simply shook his head.

Contrary to his fears, instead of an increased loathing for mortals the more he explored the Father's slipshod work, Santa's compassion for the human race grew without bound.

How could it not?

He had, after all, been granted earthly memories as Saint Nicholas, subject to every temptation he saw on display before him.

No single fix was possible. Every area of weakness reinforced all the others.

In the periphery, Aphrodite moved with a sway and guile unplanned because completely natural.

Focus.

Focus!

"Take this down, Fritz."

"Yes, Santa." Fritz stood poised over his notepad.

"Right here," Santa read off the quadrant location twice to ensure that Fritz got it right, "the tendency to judge others, to oversimplify, to stereotype, based on projections of the worst and denied parts of oneself. And near kin to tribalism and clannishness—over here, Fritz—the demonization of the other, the elevation of Us as better than a less-than-human Them. The nation state, flag waving, pride in crippling the young as war fodder. War, war, war.

"Over here, another biggie: Delusions of ownership. My stuff. My land. My home. My children. My spouse. And with the latter two, an inclination to dehumanize, to lord it over even one's loved ones—who therefore aren't really loved at all. One vast smothering security blanket. Away with all of it."

Santa's mind was already racing ahead to fixes for the areas of falter and fall he had located. But they would require intricate tinkering and he didn't want to jump to premature—and quite possibly wrong—conclusions.

Not this near the deadline.

"Jot down irrational fears, inappropriate fight-or-flight invocations, panic multiplied and distorted by mass delusion. Later we'll trace the path from these back to the tribal tendencies up above. Read off the locations, please, Fritz."

The elf complied.

"Good!

"Over here, we're back to the tightrope again, the illusion of firm ground where there's no ground at all. Overweening pride, an over-reliance on belief in the ego as anything more than a fleeting try at seemingly solid, but ultimately delusional, self-definition.

"And here, Fritz, we can clearly see the pathways from that belief to religious clinging. Note the rabid discomfort with doubt that feeds into this area, where misguided groups—clans again—create gods in their own image, answer the Big Questions in ways which reinforce their pre-existing prejudices and put down as inferior and sure-to-be-punished those who believe otherwise or who believe nothing at all about their chosen areas of delusion.

"I promise you, lads, our reshaped men and women will be comfortable to a fault with self-doubt. And others will celebrate them for it."

Santa sensed Aphrodite listening intently as she bent to her work. Admiring him, perhaps. Possibly even growing moist at picturing him—so bold and decisive a hero—in her arms, between her thighs, penetrating her as she opened to him.

Focus, dammit, focus!

"More samples, lads. Now that I know where the underlying connections are, I need a full panoply of psyches from mortals of every strip, the badly fallen right on up to those who succeed in deflecting vile tendencies. We need to examine their over-psyches and determine how they evolved over a lifetime."

With Wendy's help he rattled off names, over three score of them. Young and old. Males. Females. Those in power and those merely galumphing along in well-deserved obscurity.

Then the steady stream of psyches began, Santa as busy as ever, steeled against the ugly sights ahead but fired up by a task monumental yet manageable.

For hours he went on, until Fritz had filled over two dozen legal pads with tight scrawls reflecting with the utmost precision the discoveries the jolly old elf made along the way.

At last, Santa said, "Thank you, Fritz. Your help as always has been invaluable. Now, lads, wish your dear friend Santa god-speed. I'm going to take these notes to my office to assimilate and digest. With luck, in no more than two days, we'll have cobbled together a working model of our final design."

That brought smiles to the sea of elfin faces, and a rolling murmur of delight which rose to hearty cheers.

Santa gave out freely with gales of laughter, wishing he felt as sure inside as he pretended to feel outside.

Two days later, Santa joined Fritz and Ludwig for one more visit from Frank Worthington.

The mortal saw Santa and brightened considerably.

"That's more like it," he said. "Damn it all to hell, I always knew you existed."

Fritz had never seen the fellow so animated.

Santa beamed. "Why if it isn't little Frankie, all grown up. So good to see you, so pleased to meet the man you became."

"Wow!" Worthington teared up at Santa's embrace. "You make me feel ashamed. Sorry for the failings. But you accept me as I am, don't you? There's such warmth in your eyes."

The smile never left Santa's face. "Frankie, we need to attend to business. My worthy elves have recruited me to work on your psyche. Are you okay with that?"

"Of course! How could I say no?"

Fritz knew exactly how this mortal could say no.

But he kept mum.

Santa was the picture of unhurried efficiency.

"Now Frankie, just sit here. You've seen the psyche before. I've made my tweaks to it already, so please allow me to impose them on you. Here we go!"

The old psyche gave way to the new.

Worthington's face lit up with delight. "Oh my, that feels good."

"Tell me about, Krista, the woman you married."

The man paused, looked away as his eyes grew moist. "Oh my. Krista is . . . there are no words . . . she brings me such joy."

"Does she know that?" There was no judgment in Santa's voice.

"She will, once I get back."

Santa probed everywhere he had tinkered with the man's psyche, questioning him, prompting him, and showing Fritz and Ludwig with clear instruction where his fixes lay and how to inlay them into other psyches as they worked together in the coming days.

Frank Worthington never lost his look of wonder. He let Santa do with him what he would, addressing the red-suited elf in reverent tones. Sitting on the tall stool, his shoes sometimes tapped together like a little boy's at an ice cream parlor.

"You've done well, Frankie," said Santa. "Now I don't want you despairing. We're going to send you home, but with the psyche you came with. Very soon we'll be giving the entire human race new psyches, very much improved, modeled after this one. You won't recall being here, and we'll be softening the letdown you would otherwise feel. Just know that I love you and that everything will be all right."

Worthington looked forlorn. "I'd rather not go, if it's all the same to you."

"I know, Frankie. I'll always be with you in your heart. Seek me there."

Before the mortal could respond, Santa waved a hand and sent him back home.

Fritz laughed. "It appears we have a winner."

"We do indeed."

There was no mistaking the look of triumph on Santa's face.

Santa stewed.

Another goddamn middle-of-the-night meditation in the early hours of the second of February.

He kept his office dark, a thick, red, holiday candle maintaining a steady flame on the floor before him.

His lust for Aphrodite made it impossible for even the slowest, deepest in-breath to calm him.

So he gave in to focusing on that lust and what, if anything, he intended to do about it.

Point one: This is my body, to take pleasure in on my own terms.

Point two: Intimate physical sharing with another is just about the most wonderful activity one can engage in—second only to designing, crafting, and delivering Christmas gifts to well-behaved children.

Point three: Love is not limited in quantity. My love for Anya doesn't diminish my love for Rachel, nor vice versa. If anything, one love freely allowed makes other loves flourish.

So, even though I shouldn't have to ask permission of anyone to have fun in this way, for the sake of my marriage, I'll ask my wives' permission.

At once, that struck him wrong!

It had the potential to be hurtful.

Anya would give him a thorough verbal drubbing, as she had done when Rachel entered their lives. And Rachel, ever the mediator, might not be so hot about the idea either.

They would, he feared, see it as a threat.

"How could we hope to compete with the Goddess of Love?" they would say.

"It's not a competition," he would insist.

No way would they embrace his point of view.

Then he'd be stuck. Double damned.

He'd be forced to promise to sacrifice his erotic urges for

the sake of their marriage. And then, most assuredly, he would break his promise.

Far better to keep lust secret.

Not stir things up.

Live with turmoil inside.

Mask it as part of the greater turmoil he lived with these days, part of the ticking time bomb of fixing the human psyche.

Or he could go the French way. Have an affair on the side, his wives none the wiser or silent if they had suspicions.

But he wasn't French. His roots lay elsewhere. He was stuck, God damn it all to hell, with the Teutonic steel-rod-shoved-up-the-ass way of thinking about such matters.

Meditate, dammit!

Pump all his lust into the candle flame, sit with that desire, acknowledge its power, befriend it, honor it as a worthy enemy, dialogue with it, observe how deeply it digs its hooks into him.

Above all, commit to refraining.

Do not repress, do not restrain.

Simply refrain.

Deny it its power without erecting a melodramatic scaffolding.

Come back tomorrow to cushion and candle flame, refrain again, deny again, noting the all-consuming power of lust, thanking it, and letting it go.

For now, at least in his day-to-day life, he would do nothing.

Admit to nothing.

Steer clear of the husbandly grovel.

Continue carrying on the bare hints of a flirtation, if indeed he wasn't imagining the whole thing.

That too was possible.

Beaucoup de stürm und drang about *nada*.

Again came the upsurge, the pumped-up cock, the hot hand of the goddess leading him to her boudoir, turning to him, pressing her achingly soft lips to his, whispering crazed notions in his ear, letting fall her diaphanous gown, bringing his palms to the hip-lyre of her thighs, wafting the sweet aromas of sex into his nostrils straight to the pleasure centers of his brain.

Where am I?

Who am I?

Santa and Pan ever entwined.

He thanked his lust, released it, refocused on the candle flame, and fell victim to it again before three seconds had passed.

CHAPTER FIFTEEN
SUCCESS WITHIN REACH, IN COMES LUST

Did it surprise Fritz, ten days prior to their psyche-fixing deadline, that Santa stood before them in the workshop where they all started their day and on the spur of the moment invited them—males only, sorry, ladies—to trudge through the snow to the Chapel?

Not in the least.

For days now, he had sensed something brewing.

Toy making, despite their new recruits, had fallen even farther behind.

Santa had been working feverishly at the problem of the human psyche, but had been keeping his cards close to his chest. Fritz hadn't felt a lot of jolly coming from him lately.

And at night in the dormitory, all of them seemed to have sprouted libidos, something they had heard of in mortals but never, to their knowledge, experienced firsthand. The topic was openly bruited about in late-night bunk-to-bunk bull sessions, some new tremors alive between their legs, a floppy tube meant to keep the pee off their slippers quite often turned floppy no longer.

Ludwig had dubbed them "erections" after the way a building was erected. They were unsure what to do with these erections, not quite clear why they popped up the way they did. Their engineering minds naturally gravitated toward measuring and comparing lengths, columnar girths, and various bends and aberrations that lent unique character to each one. These stalky contraptions seemed to deflate of their own accord, typically when one's train of thought turned away from their female colleagues.

So to the Chapel in blue dawnlight over pristine snow they trudged, along familiar forest paths that never kept the imprint of slipper tracks longer than half an hour.

There lay the long flat outcropping of granite they called the Altar. All about them towered snow-draped oaks that leaned into one another to form a natural aisle. Santa stood where God the Father had married him to his wives.

"Dear friends," he began as the congregated masses of green settled down, "this won't take long, but listen carefully, please."

Urgency lived in his words, an odd mix of we have all the time in the world and we've got to resume our assigned tasks without delay.

"I thank the Father for doubling our numbers. These new elves add immeasurably to the health and vitality of our community—top tinkerers all, who move with the beauty and grace of gazelles and who have picked up and streamlined our routines with amazing speed.

"Yet they distract us . . . I do not exclude myself . . . in ways I feel impelled to explain to you. All of this confuses you, I can see that. It throws you off track. Perhaps if you understood your true origins, it would help you figure out what's going on inside you and accommodate to the new reality.

"Hear me out. What I'm about to tell you will seem fantastical.

"We were not always elves, you and I.

"Our memories of the moment of our creation are implants and are false. As hard as it is to believe, you and I were once satyrs, frolicking freely in the woods, drinking wine to great excess, and embracing a host of debaucheries. I was your satyr king, known as Pan. My wife Anya was my favorite wood nymph, though playing favorites is something I rarely did."

Fritz thrilled to hear these words, haltingly falling from Santa's lips. They seemed complete nonsense, yet there was not a doubt in Fritz's mind that Santa spoke true.

"Now, as fetching as our female elves are—and they are indeed fetching in the extreme—there is another, more deep-seated reason you find yourselves drawn to them, as compass needles are drawn to magnetic north.

"They were all wood nymphs once.

"And your lovers."

94

Ludwig's hand rose into the air.

Santa thought to ignore him, but of course didn't.

"Yes, Ludwig?"

"Beggin' yer pardon, Santa, sir, but what do you mean by 'lovers'?"

As delicately as he could, Santa launched into an explanation of mammalian reproduction, parts and how they played together, these parts and those, as well as the games and dramas, tricks and traps that human beings built around their deployment and use in the creation of babies. They, as nymph and satyrs, said Santa, had taken this delightful obsession to the heights of excess, delirious and heady those heights, highly inventive those excesses.

"Now, I could beg you to suppress that side of you. But I've learned that suppression gives more power to the urges being suppressed.

"So my advice instead is to get comfortable with it, to accept lust as part of your divinity. But also to learn patience—a patience routinely practiced—something we had no use for as woodland creatures.

"Defer your pleasures.

"Work out how your evenings are to be spent. If you wish, build yourselves cabins in the woods, places for refuge and contemplation. All I ask is that you arrive at the workshop every morning with renewed focus. While there, appreciate your female co-workers, yes. But do not divert your energies into elaborately spun fantasies that distract you from your present task."

Again Ludwig's hand shot up.

"I don't get what you mean, Santa, sir. Elaborately spun fantasies? Build cabins? For what purpose?"

Santa looked blankly at him.

Although Fritz had caught the drift of the jolly old elf's remarks, the sea of puzzled faces made it clear that Fritz was far in advance of most of the others.

Santa began slowly, then sailed into his words with great passion: "Ah dear Ludwig, do you have a female elf you speak most with, perhaps joke with, and—had we soft drinks here any more—have Coke with?"

Ludwig, rubbing his cheek, squinted up in thought. "There's Flosshilde. Yes, and Dagmar. Those two, I'd say, fill the bill."

"Well, then, pick one of them. Or pick both if you're feeling really adventurous. Take them aside—refrain, I implore you, until the end of your workday—and tell them what we've discussed here. Have this little talk in Flosshilde's hut. See if together you can come up with any ideas."

"Ideas? All right. But what if nothing occurs to us? What then?"

"Sometimes masks must be removed," said Santa. "And sometimes they must be put on."

Now, Fritz thought, Saint Nick was going all cryptic on them.

"If nothing occurs, set aside your clothing, both of you, all three of you, and see if you come up with any ideas then."

"That's my general advice for all of you.

"The critical point is that we must catch up on our toy making for next Christmas, and that those of us at work on psyches have a mere ten days to reformat the underpinnings of the human race.

"My dear friends and colleagues, please join me in praying for our success in both endeavors. And take my words to heart, for the sake of our world entire."

Except for Gregor at a distance, they removed their hats and bowed their heads as Santa's prayerful words rang out in the solemn woods, a place of peace and—Fritz began to feel it—long ago in a wooded area far distant, a place of riot and fun.

Venga slipped into the psyche factory, yet another trip to grab clones of psyches from the vast repository behind the scenes.

Santa sat at his workbench as usual, three days shy of his deadline, lost in dejection and failure. But that wasn't going to stop her from doing her best to inflict what damage she could, should his efforts find their way into the world of mortals.

He wiggled his fingers at her halfheartedly.

Venga nodded and kept walking.

"Hold on, would you?"

They were the first words he had ever spoken to her and they startled her. They seemed much too loud.

Had her cover been blown? Had he tried talking to her twin sister and pieced together her deception?

"Over here, please. I have a favor to ask."

Venga did her best to mimic her twin's walk. How should she speak? With what level of deference?

"Whatever you wish, sir."

Beads of sweat stood on his brow, no hint of a smile on his lips. Those lips were tight, close to twitching in discomfort. Something was making Santa nervous, and it sure as hell wasn't his failed work on the under-psyche.

"Can you get a message to Aphrodite? I need her advice on my latest effort. Won't it wait till morning, you might wonder. Well, no, it won't. It's a question that might insult her husband, but which I need to have answered."

"No message delivery required, Santa. The goddess sleeps in the open, freely exposed to view. And she feels no violation if one approaches her as she sleeps. We golden girls sometimes go to her en masse or one at a time. She never startles awake. She welcomes us, whatever our need. That's just her way."

"Ah, good," said Santa. "Very nice." He rose shakily from his stool, reluctance in every move. "Guide me to her, golden one. What's your name?"

"Kind sir, my name isn't important. We're all pretty interchangeable, here to serve Hephaestus only. This way, please."

And she led him back to the bower—soft-scented with wafts of jasmine—in which the Goddess of Love slept, her bed draped in see-through lace from the tops of the bedposts. Pointing the way, Venga lifted her finger to her lips and withdrew, savoring the look of delight and consternation on his face.

Gregor was going to love this!

***

Santa marveled at his surroundings.

They were still inside this heavenly building, he and the sleeping goddess, yet there was no sense of being inside at all.

Were it not for the path he had taken, illumined by a muted glow upon moss, he would have thought they were in a moonlit forest, the temperature perfect for little or no clothing.

"These woods were my choice for tonight," she said, fully awake. Her words caressed his ears as lightly as a soft breeze.

She raised herself on one elbow. "Come sit by me."

He had been nervous. Guilt had been eating at him for the trespass he was about to commit. He had been berating himself for being crazy mad insane, for being ready to sacrifice all he held dear, in the name of dry, meaningless lust.

But as she spoke, as she laid exceptionally light eye contact upon him, all of that dropped away.

Her nightgown highlighted her nakedness beneath, nothing at all hidden really.

Excitation raced through Santa's body, thrills and blood and high imaginings. True it was, his penis rose thick and urgent behind his trouser buttons. But there was no shame there, nor any cause for shame, nature taking its intended course when in the presence of the Goddess of Love.

"Is your husband—?"

"He never disturbs me at night. Sit. Tell me what's on your mind."

"Yes, of course." His voice was no longer awkward, as it had been with the golden girl. It held and exuded full confidence, full Santa joy and generosity and love, full Pan lechery and grasping, neither persona warring with the other.

He parted the drapes, held them aside, and settled in as best his erection allowed, sitting nearby but not touching her.

"You're simply stunning."

She smiled in thanks.

"Could we try it just once? There'd be no harm in that. No need to tell my wives. They know who I used to be. It surely wouldn't surprise them if they found out. But why complicate things?"

She nodded at his stream of words, not in the least surprised. Bemusement played about her lips.

"I inform every act of love," she said, sidestepping his direct approach. "Love of all kinds. The erotic kind of course, but others too. Your love for innocent girls and boys, for example. I weave through all of it. When you engage in erotic play with Anya and Rachel, they are in me and I am in them. There's no need to crave me in the flesh."

She wasn't judging him. But she was most decidedly turning him down.

Hard to get?

An act?

"Your husband told me you wanted to jump my bones, or at least that you'd expressed an interest."

"Hephaestus said that?"

"In so many words."

She laughed. Her laughter made madness pound in Santa's body. "I may have said so in an idle moment. But I certainly didn't expect him to share it with you.

"Truth is, I'm always making love to everything in a muted way. I am love. So I know what you'd be like, and it would be delightful. But I've already had you vividly in my heart and soul and in my mind, which is quite adept at conjuring in delicious detail such scenarios."

"How wonderful," said Santa. "But I haven't had you!"

She touched his hand, a first direct electric touch of skin upon skin. He had to look past her face, past her perfectly coiffed angel hair, not into her eyes, lest he spend his love, thick, wet, and abrupt.

"Your lack of imagination, my dear," she mocked, "isn't my problem. In any case, no thanks. You flatter me, but there's no way this will happen. Trust me."

His absence of regret surprised him.

It was enough to be this close to her, to feel love's touch on the back of his hand, to know—and truly to feel—that she lived in every act of love, holding it in her sweet body, blessing it, blessing both the giver of love and the receiver.

"Thank you," he said, and meant it, his voice a blend harmonious of boyish Santa and ravishing Pan.

Visions of Aphrodite so consumed him that when he came to himself, he was sitting at the workbench, no memory of having found his way back.

Again at his night post in the psyche factory, Santa looked up and saw the golden girl approaching him.

Her breasts seemed larger and more inviting this time, as indeed they were. For Venga had complete pneumatic control over her body—all the golden girls did, but she alone had ever exercised it—and knew how to use it to excite the lust of males and females alike.

She drew nearer.

"Did you find the Goddess of Love, Santa?"

"I did. Please, pretty one, tell me your name."

"Oh all right. I'll whisper it."

As he sat at his workbench—an under-psyche open to probing a hand's breadth away—the body that had seemed as cool as amber sidled up to him, furnace-hot. Her honeyed breath tickled the soft shell of his ear. "I forget. Who cares? Touch me."

Fire flared in Santa's libido.

Already roused by Aphrodite's inaccessible beauty, he cupped the golden girl's buttocks in his hands and drew her close, his erection thickening below.

"Such a lovely face," he said.

What madness is this? Stop it at once!

But stop he did not.

Not until he had kissed her, felt the molten gold of her tongue in his mouth; the tug at his buttons as she freed his cock, gripped it, encircling and pulling at it to thicken it further; the soft-spun fleece above her moist labia as he fingered her and caught the catch-breaths she released.

Santa swept the under-psyche off the workbench and hoisted the golden girl upon it, spreading wide her thighs and tonguing her labia into full flower. Their taste bore no hint of the metallic, but lived in the wonder of warm honey and the

100

promise of world-changing ecstasy.

This was all he would need to save the world.

One quick fuck with this miraculous creature—not quick, no, but lingering inside magic time—would be sufficient. Their shared climax would sweep the globe and eradicate every trace of human insanity.

Santa was on the verge of touching his cock tip to Venga's vulva when there upsurged the will to resist.

I'll fail if I do this.

I'll miss my deadline.

And I'll have betrayed my wives.

He set her on her feet and buttoned up, the fabric taut over his erection.

"I'm sorry, sweetheart. You are a true temptation, but I cannot do this. Be on your way."

Something peculiar flashed across her face, a mask briefly dropped, then back in place as if nothing at all had changed.

And she was gone.

It happened so swiftly, Santa thought he must have imagined it. But that niggling little doubt lingered, stubbornly refusing to dissipate, as he did his best to resume his work.

But Santa's best wasn't good enough.

Time and again, his efforts were derailed by lust he was unable to shut out.

Finally he threw up his hands and beelined to the meditation cushion in his office.

Even there, his efforts proved ineffectual. A blither of unbridled desires attacked him from all directions, no peace where peace had always come to comfort him.

Once he had placed and activated the new psyches, would he cheat on his wives with this golden girl?

There was no time to do it now. Time was precious. He beat himself over even sitting here in meditation, doing absolutely nothing productive.

He wanted to remain faithful, keep no secrets from Rachel and Anya, especially not sexual secrets arising in his Pan self. It had been a terrible time, back when he had stepped out on

Anya with the Tooth Fairy. To revert was unthinkable. Yet it plagued his thoughts.

Then his lust affixed itself to the visions of his dear wives and he had to have them now!

He rushed to his bedroom, where they slumbered still in one another's arms. He stripped himself naked, then tore away the blanket and sheets. His wives, used to such goings on, awakened. He made short work of Anya's nightgown and Rachel's blue silk nightie. Then they dove with gusto into the maelstrom of desire that carried their husband on.

Santa was both present to his wives and not present at all, as flesh slid and pounded against flesh.

At first, he brought Aphrodite into their threesome, imagining her taste—a mix of almonds, vanilla, honey, and cardamom—as she wrapped the three of them in her loving limbs. She made it all frantically superb, the fluids amped up in flavor, the labia more slippery, the clits and nipples harder, the vaginal sleeves rich with a warm grip-and-release.

Then he substituted the golden girl and that made everything rank and vile.

Drop her.

Back to Aphrodite.

Conjuring up her image did not feel like cheating at all. Indeed, Santa began drawing her into a shared sexual fantasy. Rachel and Anya took to this at once, each in turn adding her take on what the Goddess of Love would do to them, and they to her.

Never the golden girl, then.

Not in fantasy and not in real life.

His instincts told Santa she was a significant threat to his marriage.

Which made her, of course, all the more alluring.

Madness!

The twelfth of February.

Since the meeting in the Chapel eight days before, Santa had worked around the clock, no sleep at all, no joyrides on Lucifer's back, no breaks for walking, no nada—except of course for his brief visit to Aphrodite and his near seduction by the golden girl.

The psyche factory bustled with activity during the day but was dead silent all night, save for the comings and goings of that one golden girl—always a quick wave from her, nothing more, and when he saw her during the day, she took no particular notice of him.

Squelch it, he thought, pleased at his success.

Thirteen days before, he had cracked the code for Frank Worthington, a significant triumph.

But most of the test mortals' over-psyches didn't fit at all with the prototype he had come up with for the under-psyche.

Tweak and test, tweak and test.

The Father God's engineering of the original under-psyche was an infernal quagmire, stubbornly resistant to change.

Santa's fix would seem firmly positioned, say, in the area of extreme xenophobia. Yet all it took was one hint of a suggestion of a slur from some friend, or a misreported incident in the media, and the fix would crumble, the old structure emerging once more like a butterfly from its chrysalis.

But on this day, as dawn broke two days prior to the fatal tipping point, Santa smiled.

This under-psyche was the one.

It passed every test with every human being of the hundreds sampled.

There was nothing wrong with his master tinkering. But there was plenty wrong with the distance he had maintained. Unbeknownst to himself, he had still been resisting close contact with adult folly. In the end, all it had taken was to peer with compassion into the depths of each tormented psyche he experimented with, find the lost innocent child inside, and be sure that connections from the under-psyche to that child were as strong as possible.

He had found just the right mix of hand waving, re-engineering, and Santa-like generosity of spirit to be certain at last of this prototype.

As his work crew began to stream into the psyche factory, simultaneous with the appearance of the golden girls and

103

7

the immortals they served, Santa beckoned to his wife and stepdaughter.

"Be patient one moment, lads," he said. The relief in his voice was reflected in their faces and in the brief glances they exchanged.

He took Wendy and Rachel out onto the commons. "I have good news," he said, turning slowly to take in this glorious day and the magnificence and wonder of the community it was his good fortune to be a part of.

"Let it be what I hope for, Daddy."

"Tell us, dear."

"It is indeed, Wendy," he said, tears of joy standing in his eyes. "I have at long last a solid prototype."

Wendy yelped with joy and threw herself into her father's arms. "I knew you could do it!"

Rachel joined their embrace, giving her husband a joyous kiss and a smile you could take to any eternal bank and cash in for a fortune in gems and gold.

"It's time—not a moment to lose—to consider our delivery mechanism, the pre-placement of the under-psyches and the moment of the switchover."

Wendy did her best to calm herself. "You're right. We'll celebrate later. You and I can deliver them, can't we?"

"As much as I'd like to, it's best I stay at the psyche factory in case any emergencies crop up. You should definitely be involved though, in both phases of the operation."

Wendy's eyes widened. She snapped her fingers. "What about the Easter Bunny? He did such a great job with the chocolate eggs made from the Divine Mother's milk when we battled the homophobes. I'm sure he still has his magic knapsack."

Santa noticed Rachel's feint at a wince which, to her credit, she squelched at once.

"Great idea," he said.

"I'm off to the gingerbread house. I'll summon the archangel. I'll also request the Son's presence, though that's probably a long shot."

"Yes," said Santa, "we'll need Michael's help and the

Father's permission too. Let's aim for their placement tomorrow. Pick a time that's best for you and for the Easter Bunny."

"Will he do it, do you think?"

"He'll be ecstatic. He's one excitable bunny, and this is going to excite him, I have no doubt."

"I'm off then. Wish me luck."

Rachel kissed her on the cheek. "Good luck, dear. I'm so proud of you."

"Ditto, Mom. But counting our chickens will come later."

Santa clasped Rachel to him as Wendy raced away through the snow. "Let's go tell the elves."

"Then Anya," she said.

"Yes."

They turned to the psyche factory, Santa wondering how pleased Aphrodite would look when she heard the news.

CHAPTER SIXTEEN
SAVIORS, PLOTS,
AND PLANS

By the time Wendy reached the gingerbread house, Michael and the Son were already there. Merely her intent to summon them had sufficed.

"Good," she said. "You honor us, dear divine beings, with your presence. Do we need to concern ourselves with God's buy-in? Is He still with us?"

"He is, sweetheart," said the Son.

Wendy was all business. "We'll need to summon the Easter Bunny and fill him in."

"Michael, please fetch the furry one."

"No sooner said." The archangel vanished.

"I'll be taking part in the deliveries as well, if you don't mind."

"Mind? How could I?" asked Wendy.

"Not in the placement though. At the switchover. I'll absorb the defective psyches as they're swapped out. It would be well, too, to offer my humble blessing as each new psyche is implanted."

Before Wendy could thank him again, there before them in a flurry of joy stood the Easter Bunny. Michael resumed his place beside the Son.

"Oh, my," said the Easter Bunny, "the zesty air of the North Pole, and dear sweet Wendy, still looking all of nine. How old are you really?"

"Twenty-something inside. No time for that now. Day after Valentine's Day, ask me again and we can linger for hours over that question." Truth be told, it was a tender subject for her. She had no objection to looking like a nine-year-old, but it did put the joys of adulthood and parenting forever out of reach.

"Of course. The good archangel here gave me the gist with the utmost urgency and swooped me up into a whirlwind.

106

A very pleasant and exciting trip, if I may say so. Thank you, Mister Michael, sir!"

"Observe," said Wendy, directing his attention to the wall. "I've muted the impact of the impending human catastrophe a little, as your heart is, I know, very tender. Observe, please, what will happen if we do nothing."

"Dear me! Good heavens!" said the Easter Bunny. His face would have turned white were it not already a riot of shock-white fur. "But however do you intend to avert such a massive disaster?"

Wendy wiped away the images.

His hind feet thumped furiously on the carpet. "Sorry, I—"

The Easter Bunny lost for a moment the ability to speak, so overcome by grief was he at the terrible transformation the world of mortals would soon undergo. "Alas, my dear darling human race, to suffer such loss. Never to realize their full potential for good, for love, for joy, for—"

Wendy stopped him.

She raised his hopes, filling him in on their progress at the psyche factory, their plans to set new psyches in place and to swap out the old, worldwide.

"But where do I come in?"

"You'll play a critical role," Wendy said. "I'll map out our path around the planet and a team of elves here will slip the next psyche through the Universal Womb into your knapsack. All you need do is pass it to me for placement. Then we'll go on to the next. Quite simple tasks, but critical to our success."

"Oh yum, yum, yum!" he said, then abruptly cut his joy short. "Two questions. Why isn't Santa delivering them in his sleigh from his pack? And can magic time be stretched that far? Aren't we talking about—oh let's see—over seven billion placements and over seven billion eventual swappings out?"

"We are," said Wendy. "But Michael assures me that given our efficiency in laying out our route, we can deliver everything, with room to spare, in fewer than five seconds of real time.

"As for Santa, he needs to be at the ready in the psyche factory in case mishaps arise, both as regards placement and activation. Besides, you did such a marvelous job of delivering those chocolate eggs to the bedsides of homophobes, I'm sure your steel-trap mind won't fail us."

The Easter Bunny's eyes lit up. "Oh I really must see this psyche factory. Can we go there now? And oh yes indeedy, thank you, darling Wendy, for that vote of confidence. It's just my way. Attention to detail is all important. But you and Santa already knew that."

"I'll show you the factory sometime," she said, in a bit of a hurry. "Now though, we need to drop in on Santa, scope out our plan, get his approval, and start making it happen. We're talking about tomorrow for these placements, after all."

"Oh of course—"

"Then let's be off."

Wendy took the lead, followed by the Easter Bunny and their heavenly guests, across the commons to the workshop.

Santa welcomed the entourage into his office, the elves agape at the presence of the Holy Savior and an archangel as they passed through the workshop, and closed the door.

"Wendy," said Santa, "it's your show. Tell us how we need to proceed."

"I'll summarize," she said, taking the floor.

Out of respect for his guests—at least the heavenly ones—her stepfather stood.

The Easter Bunny's presence he tolerated.

"I've mapped out where every human being will be at noon Greenwich Meridian Time on Valentine's Day. That includes those born seconds before then, but not the hapless stillborns. I nearly excluded those fated to die shortly after activation time, but decided they too should enjoy a brief moment of soul transplantation.

"To these locations on the globe we'll pin the new psyches, put in place tomorrow and substituted for the old psyches the day after."

"Oh this is such joy," said the Easter Bunny. "To be a part of saving the human race! But won't they see the waiting psyches, bump into them, be alarmed at their presence, not knowing what they are? And might your predictions as to placement need to shift if, by free choice, some of them change their plans and are in a spot other than the one you expect them to show up in? And, oh my, what if nefarious creatures have been working behind the scenes to foil your plans, such as a certain fairy it were best not to name lest I bruise our divine visitors' ears?"

Santa bristled at the Easter Bunny's interruptions. "All of these concerns I'm sure Wendy has taken under advisement. Let her continue."

"Beg pardon." His ears stood slightly less erect than a moment before. "I'm so excited, and I want to be of help, in whatever—"

"Yes, yes, we know." Santa put a finger to his lips, doing his best not to unleash his temper.

"I've spoken with my wondrous stepfather here," continued Wendy, her concern for humanity a joy to Santa's heart, "and everything's at the ready to clone every last living psyche, replace their under-psyches, reconnect the over-psyches to their new foundation, and assure ourselves they're in the precise order that conforms to the route the Easter Bunny and I will take tomorrow. Each newborn psyche, as it comes off the assembly line, will also be so treated and slotted into its proper place in the long sequence of clones. Each psyche, as it reaches the head of that sequence, will be directed into the Universal Womb and appear in our furry friend's magic knapsack. He'll hand it to me and I will set it in place."

She paused to let it all sink in.

"Is everyone in agreement?"

The Son's beaming smile said all he needed to say, and Michael admiration boiled down to, "Entirely."

"Oh but what if—?" began the Easter Bunny. "Ah, never mind. We haven't time to touch on my many anxieties, I know. I get so het up. It's just my nature. So I think we ought to get cracking, as the mortals say."

"Indeed we ought," said Santa.

And cracking they got.

Up heavenward through the ceiling of Santa's office

drifted Michael and the Son, signaling their blessings with their raised right hands.

"Be ready," said Wendy.

"I will," said the Easter Bunny and swirled about into a vanishing point.

"To the psyche factory," said Santa. "We haven't a moment to spare."

When Quint and Gronk bumbled back to report Santa's triumph in perfecting a painless reconnection and reintegration of each over-psyche with his final version of the under-psyche, the Tooth Fairy lashed out at Venga. She gripped the squatting golden girl by the throat and rose into the air above the shore, her other hand clawed into Venga's belly.

"That fat little red-suited black-booted fuck is busy making seven billion copies of his masterwork, and you're still waving your hands over a damned pile of psyches on the beach. I will have results!"

Venga, not bothering to fight back—she had no need to breathe, come right down to it—glared a glare so ferocious that the Tooth Fairy caught full in the face the chill blast of death. But she maintained her grip, squeezing harder than ever.

I'll kill her now, she thought.

I'll swallow the bitch whole, shit out cascades of doubloons, and bury them full fathom five in the sea.

Who the hell does she think she is?

And in front of my youngest imp too?

She threw the insolent creature to the shore.

Venga resumed her squatting position as though nothing had happened.

"Now that Pan has finally lifted his hand from his chess piece," she said, "I'll steal one last copy of that precious under-psyche and bring it back. It can't be too far off what I've experimented with so far. You'll see. I've managed to sheath his most critical fixes in transparent sleeves of reversal, booby traps poised to be sprung as soon as the swap-out occurs, irrevocably worsening things worldwide."

110

"If you fail, Quint will hurtle you back to Tartarus into the loathsome arms of Hades."

Venga rose beside the mortal psyches and that of the Sky God. She stepped confidently up to Adrasteia and looked her in the eye—not challenging her, but with sheer womanly lust. "You're so sexy when you're angry. And you're angry most of the time. I'd much rather be the object of your attention than Hades', and I intend doing nothing that stands in the way of that goal."

She looked at Quint, then at his mother. "A visit to Gregor, the theft of a few clones, and I'll be back to firm up our plans."

So saying, Venga rose into the air and sped away.

"One day, I'll murder that saucy little piece of ass," said the Tooth Fairy to her son. "See if I don't."

When she reached for Quint's erection, he parried. Her arm bruised at his deflection.

Was there no end to the shaming? she wondered. *Do I really have to kill them both?*

CHAPTER SEVENTEEN
DIRTY ROTTEN SCHEMERS,
PSYCHES PLACED

Moments before, Gregor had left his post at the stable door and slipped into a blush-red nightgown and tassled nightcap.

He tucked himself in for a lonely snooze and was just about to blow out the lantern on his nightstand when—glory be—his golden friend Venga peered in at the door.

She didn't give so much as a rap about his privacy, nor did she ask his permission to enter, but boldly waltzed in.

Porous boundaries about that one, to be sure.

Run away from her, he thought. *Keep a couple of leagues distant always.*

Then his little head started to speak, and it easily drowned out the big one.

Permission? He wouldn't have denied her that.

Point of fact, he would never deny her anything.

"Listen up," she said. Then she stared at what he was wearing and changed course. "That get-up makes you look like an idiot. When you and I take over, no more nightgowns for you. Leather's more your style. Leather and chains."

Beneath said nightgown, concealed by his covers, that damned stalk of flesh was sticking up again. The hairs on his neck too.

Once a satyr, eh?

Lovely.

An utter lack of discipline. And pride in that lack. Drunkenness. Debauchery. God damn the unsaintly Saint Nicholas for filling their minds with such alas-now-obviously-truthful rot.

It explained the frequency of this accursed flesh-rise whenever some beskirted elfette—he refused to honor these bimbos with the name 'elf'—sashayed her goddamned femininity near the stables or, God help him, came a-calling, whole gaggles of them, to pet, feed, and fawn over Santa's reindeer.

They had no notion they had been wood nymphs. Not them. But Gregor could smell the moss, loam, and tree bark on them. He caught a whiff of the arousing scent they carried in their bones, cover it up how they might.

"You won't believe," he said, "what Mister Big Belly told the male elves in the woods."

"What?"

He told her.

"Oh I believe it all right." She raised the covers and eased in beside him, sliding a hand up under the hem of his nightshirt. "Let's see if I can make *you* believe it, right down to the root and fundament of your first and second chakras. I'll bet I can."

And indeed she did, compromising to the max his stalwart stance against unruly passions and bringing to the fore the rude red riot of his inner satyr.

Moreover, while Venga groped and stroked him, memories of what the other elves (he having held back from partaking, in an absurd clinging to so-called righteous behavior) had done to Santa's wife Anya—with her eager consent no less—trickled at first, then flooded, into visual and olfactory recall.

"Do tell," she said, during a lovemaking lull. "O my vicious little sweetie pie, you're right to grin.

"That's pure Santacidal ammo you've got there, at its most wounding. Capture and keep those memories. We're going to need them."

"Mmmmmph," he said.

'That's right, Gregor. Bite that nipple. Do tongue-swirls around it. Suck on it. Take Venga's sweet honey-milk down your gullet. That, and power without limit, can and shall be yours!"

At the same hour that Gregor was grumbling over losing his cherry to Venga, Quint and the Tooth Fairy were engaged in their own variation on the Sublime Nasty.

Ever vigilant in matters erotic, the Tooth Fairy had seen at long last a certain look she had always hoped to see in Quint's eye.

It was time to clear the beach.

"Haul your ungainly ass over here, Gronk."

"Yes, Mother?"

By God, her fucking offspring sickened her.

"Tomorrow, you will shadow Wendy and the Easter Bunny, mapping in that devious little mind their exact route as they place the new psyches."

"I can do that."

"Cut the crap, of course you can. I have no idea how you're able to keep such stores of information in that duller than dull brain, but you proved capable before, so I have no doubt you can do it again."

Over her damned imp's shoulder, Quint's cock stood as thick and tall as ever. But this time, the slither of his eyes across her body made his intent clear.

She seized Gronk's arm and shook him.

"Ouch, that hurts!"

"It'll hurt a whole lot more if you disobey my orders. Find your brothers, herd them, keep them as far from me as possible until tomorrow. If any of them shows his fuck-ugly face before then, I'll savage him and you both, over and over, until I've punched a tunnel into your thick skulls that will make the penetrative power of my words clearly felt."

Before Gronk could eke out a sufficiently mewling response, she swung him about—once, twice, thrice—and let him go, spinning through drizzled rain toward the beach his siblings favored.

"Now then," said the Tooth Fairy, trading fire for fire with her youngest imp's eyes, "Is something on your mind, sonny boy?"

"Quite a lot, yes."

Quint took himself in hand, the first time he had done that in her presence, tugging slow and sensual. His gaze upon her never broke.

Her imps were all oily little shits, which was one reason— though not the primary one—she gripped them in a vise lock when they needed roughing up.

"Let Momma help."

She double-fisted him, twisting and twirling his well-oiled

prick from tip to testicles. A current almost electric coursed up her arm, hardening her nipples and clit and raising a ruddy glow on her skin.

Cool customer, this Quint.

No signs of pleasure disturbed the laconic placidity of his face.

But as she worked at him, the mystery of the wafer-thin coins in the sand resolved itself. Several of them spilled from the slit in his penis, a slow trickle of gold disks in easy succession, flipping away and tumbling soundlessly to the sand.

Now she understood the piles of coins in his cave.

"Turn over," he said without urgency.

"Impudent boy," she said. "Lie on your back."

"I said, turn over!"

Then he grabbed her, flew her in his powerful arms above the strand, and spun her to face away from him.

"How dare you?" She flailed about, scratching at his face there in the air.

Quint was having none of it. He grabbed her again and brought her back the way he wanted her, his left arm locked about her waist, his right hand wrenching her hair back with such violence that her neck bones cracked and her necklace of bloody teeth clattered and rapped twice against her breasts.

Tiny coins hit the small of her back and tickled the flesh between her buttocks, falling away below.

Then he began to ease into her anus, his erection's vibrations melting any resistance her sphincter might have offered. Acceptance pure and simple tightened about him as he progressed.

In every other way, however, she fought like a hell-hound, tearing ineffectually at his arm, reaching back to grip his neck but not finding it, flailing her legs. Yet Quint had complete control of their progress through the air.

She suddenly had none.

"Let me go!" she bellowed.

"When we're finished," he said, that unbelievable calm carrying his voice.

115

Those words changed the game.

He was rough, yes, and rapine.

But he wasn't trying to triumph over her, no power struggle here.

Just ferocious sex.

On his terms.

He knew her protests were hollow.

Now she did too.

Still, it was a grand and exciting game, this feint at resistance. So resist she did, her words failing her and turning into the sexual growl of a wildcat being neck-scruffed while her mate thrust into her from behind.

At long last, Quint gave out with a surging yawp of pleasure. His coin spurts coursed rapidly through her intestines, coiling about and about, internal clatter at the corners of the coil.

When they rose up into her stomach, she felt them changing, melting, reconstituting as bone matter and flying up beyond that, taking their reverse course.

From her mouth, as her lover pumped and pumped, tiny white teeth shot forth and fell to the beach.

She watched as they stippled the sand, taking root and growing into delicate sand-flowers, bone-white with fragile spines.

She took huge gulps of air. Then the vomitus surged anew, and soon the beach was covered in beauteous white blossoms, a sight that made her scream for love and joy.

On the thirteenth of February, as pre-dawn reds and purples smeared the skies above the commons, the Easter Bunny appeared right on schedule, his silk-and-velvet knapsack high on his back, its strap like a bandoleer across his chest.

Wendy took up Galatea's reins. "Hop in, sir."

At once Santa collared him, whispering through hot-chocolate-scented breath, "Don't you dare."

The Eater Bunny blinked, then gave a nod, though he had no idea what Santa's problem was.

Something damning, from the look on his face.

"If you don't mind, sweet girl, I'd rather trail along behind you on my own steam," he said. "I'm so used to a certain freedom of movement. But fear not, I'll keep up."

"Oh, all right." Wendy nearly clucked her tongue. "You and Daddy!"

Her moms gave her encouraging hugs. The elves in mixed pairs thronged her, babbling excited farewells. Even sour-faced Gregor relaxed his grump a teensy bit as he stood nearby for the sendoff.

"I'm so proud of you, sweetheart," said Santa. "Once you've put the psyches in place, our success is assured. In some ways, yours is the most important task of all."

"I love you, Daddy. It's a team effort and I'm thrilled to play my part."

With that, she lightly rein-slapped Galatea's flank and was off, slanting sharply up into the winter sky, the Easter Bunny close behind. When she enwrapped both sleigh and bunny in magic time, her family and the community of elves froze in place.

As he zoomed along, he kept his focus on Wendy's sleigh, maintaining a distance of twenty feet. Into their marathon journey about the globe they sped, models of efficient delivery.

Wendy directed her sleigh here and there, spoke a mortal's name, and held out her hands.

At each name, the Easter Bunny reached back to catch the tiny psyche that sprang from his knapsack. Full-sized it grew between his paws and from there he tossed it to Wendy, who affixed it to the air.

Sometimes, a psyche filled part of a space occupied by an object which, when the great transformation came, would no longer be there.

And sometimes, in the case of submarine crews, scuba divers, or just-wiped-out surfboarders, the psyches were placed underwater, a fun thing that.

Wendy's accuracy he trusted implicitly.

Tomorrow at the appointed time, these psyches and the mortals that would house them would coincide.

Of that he had no doubt.

In rare cases, the intended body was already there, most

often victims of coma lying abed like Vera Wells of Topeka, Kansas in her room at St. Francis Hospital.

"Vera," said Wendy, "awakens next fall. She'll need her new psyche then. This woman has an astounding future ahead of her."

"Say more!"

"Once we're done. Let's press on."

And so they did.

Sometimes the Easter Bunny grew so excited he had to leap into the air and zigzag all around Wendy and her sleigh, sweeping like a crazed maniac through the night sky. Monumental the gift they were giving the human race. And he, humble bunny, was blessed to be a part of it. It made him zing and zizzle inside, like . . . well, like nothing he could describe. But pre-explosive ecstasy came close.

Always, Wendy would rein him in, bemused, yes, but understanding.

Such a sweet child!

Their most bizarre set of placements occurred in the airspace over Bonn, Germany.

"Why are we—?"

"Just feed me psyches, okay?"

They had of course populated other aircrafts-to-be high above the earth, the psyches roaming the aisles, manning the cockpit, or lined up in serried ranks in what, tomorrow, would be seats. But this jet was clearly canted at a heartbreaking angle less than half a mile above thick forest, not a landing strip in sight.

Wendy slotted the psyches in the air—men, women, children, and infants in car seats—no evidence of the panic fated to overwhelm them all.

As they wrapped up, Wendy said somberly, "We've placed psyches for mortals not yet born, who will have taken their first breath by noon tomorrow. And we've skipped over those destined to die by then. But these poor people will still have a few moments of life left. They deserve this gift, however brief. Let's move on."

They covered much ground then, finishing the task of

setting seven billion plus psyches in place.

These souls in waiting looked superb and smelled even better, like hollyhocks, peppermint, and freshly ground coffee beans, wrapped in the aroma of salt sea air coming off breakers hitting a beach.

The Easter Bunny anticipated with near unbearable glee the miracle due on the morrow. Yet he remained focused on the task, not missing a beat in their work together.

As they concluded, they took one quick low swirl around the globe, thrilled at the pattern of lights made by the waiting psyches.

"Thank you, dear friend," said Wendy, relief in her voice. "Our part in Santa's gift is done!"

CHAPTER EIGHTEEN
DESPOLIATION IN DETAIL

While Wendy and the Easter Bunny were spreading joy-in-potentia across the globe, Venga agonized over her clone of Santa's perfected under-psyche.

"Back off!" she shouted over and over at the Tooth Fairy. That brought on ferocious attacks, in part a fight to the death, in part a sexual come-on.

After umpteen scorings and mutilations—mutually inflicted, instantly healed—the Tooth Fairy hovered high above the shore, feigning disinterest.

Venga alternated a love-hate for her with a lust for power. As she toiled, she conjured visions of the North Pole under her control. Far from distracting her, those visions sharpened the focus of her efforts.

Santa's last and best under-psyche, damn him, had undergone changes radical enough to force Venga to reengineer her methods of concealment.

She set the Father God's original botch of an under-psyche beside this new one, whose vast improvements were stark and clear. Her deadline loomed too near to reverse or nullify all of Santa's tweaks and revisions. The most significant half dozen, however, would fall to her attack.

Venga worked feverishly against the clock.

Fear of failure.

Acknowledge it and let it go.

So too, pride in the dance of her fingers above the clone. Before being thrown down to Tartarus, she had watched Hephaestus at work and learned her lessons well, how to perfect the join of upper and lower, how to repeat it with precision and exactitude every time.

She placed her booby traps with care, camouflaging them, as before, in convincing mockeries of Santa's rejiggerings. A deft twist of the hand to the left undid her changes, a right twist restored them. Moving from one psyche to the next in quick circumnavigation, she gestured her changes in and was on her way.

If she, Gronk, and Adrasteia could escape detection during the swaps performed along Wendy's route, it was simply a matter of keeping the curious girl's nose out of future projections until tomorrow's fate-sealing switcheroo.

Gregor could help with that.

The tooth-eating bitch above her flew nearer.

Look anguished. Throw up your hands. Make her think you're failing. Get her goat.

Why bother? It was enough to keep up the conflict, tussle with her in rough sex, make her think they were on the same team, that she would extract power from Zeus's immortal psyche and channel it into the Tooth Fairy's psyche instead of her own.

When it was too late, she would hurl the Tooth-Fairy-No-Longer down to Tartarus into the odious arms of Hades for all eternity.

Wrap Gregor around her little finger.

Set about further reshaping the world.

Cause whole heaps of mayhem.

And have a grand old time wallowing in chaos.

Sweet!

As she and the Easter Bunny approached the North Pole, Wendy swept away the mantle of magic time. At once, furious blasts of snow buffeted them, making it hard to breathe and covering her sleigh with swirls of white.

But when they pierced the protective bubble that enclosed Santa's community, the flakes turned light and gentle, the temperature mild.

Her sleigh's runners kissed virgin snow, easing to a soft hissed stop. All around them, the winter sun sent swirls of diamonds up from the drifts. Clusters of pine trees burned brilliant green, casting shadows of dark purple across the snowscape.

The Easter Bunny followed, his back feet touching down beside Galatea. "Why are we stopping here?"

"This day is so magnificent, isn't it?" said Wendy, a smile as wondrous as the sunlight. "What's more, you and I have performed miracles. Before Santa and the elves swarm us—as satisfying as that's going to feel—I thought we might pause to consider what we've done together."

"Goody!" he exclaimed, clapping his paws, though the only sounds produced were the faint click of claws and the soft brush of fur against fur.

"So prepare yourself for a quick jaunt through the futures of nearly everyone whose lives we've touched. Don't get dizzy. Try not to fix on anyone in particular. Go with the flow, catch glimpses, and move on."

With that, Wendy poured forth a stream of scenes against the sky, showing the kindnesses destined to be unleashed. No longer were men and women plagued with selfishness nor with the clutch of fears that kept their worthiest instincts deadened and shut down. Rather, their love for others—even for those they might once have considered strangers—came surging forth.

People still stood before arrays of moral choices, but the easy fast-food temptations were routinely brushed aside. Shoplifting came thudding to a halt, along with bullying, gossiping, sitting in judgment, and obsessing over objects of lust. Too, the projection of pleasures to come and the incessant replay of past events, at the expense of living fully now, no longer held such a tight grip on the human mind.

Wendy lingered over the lives of those Santa had examined in the psyche factory.

She watched as the couple from Colmar, Jacques and Dominique LaFramboise, immediately started to make plans to separate. But as swiftly, they saw one another in a new light. Their wedded drudgery lifted. When their daughter dropped in, she found that they had not only reconciled but had taken to one another as they had in their youth. Even the steps they took to sever their extramarital connections went beautifully awry. For together they recognized the wonderfulness Pierre and Yvonne had provided—the playfulness and the joy—and brought those extra sensual connections into their marriage as a delicious foursome.

"Oh that's so French," exclaimed the Easter Bunny.

Wendy laughed. "Let's look in on the gentleman from Akron, shall we?"

Willard Frist was also destined to change overnight. Wendy watched him rein in his sales people, though they too had changed and were no longer a problem. For the first time in his life, Frist adored children and strove to make even better educational toys. He gave out generous bonuses to his employees. Why, he even stepped away from his type-A behavior and launched a search for a compatible mate to spend his days with.

"He wasn't always this way?"

"No indeed. He was a regular Scrooge."

Finally, Wendy turned to Gillian Barnes, a London snob no more. Conscience and responsibility would bloom in her. She would seek out ways to make her wealth useful to others. She would turn curious about the world, become a volunteer, set up endowments, get her hands dirty, clean up her life, and see, with a clarity that would startle her, the divine spark in all people regardless of wealth or class.

"Such a lovely lady."

"Soon to be so, yes," said Wendy.

She swept the scenes away. The pristine beauty of the North Pole again enveloped them.

"Gloriosky!" exclaimed the Easter Bunny, delirious with joy.

"Don't spoil the surprise by telling the others about this, okay? Let them wait."

"But—"

"No buts!"

"Oh, all right. But I'm going to bail right here. Even if I said nothing, my face would betray us. My work is done anyway. I say we separate."

Wendy agreed, delighted at his innocence and his thoughtfulness.

Waving and blowing a kiss, he shot skyward.

Beneath his words, for reasons unknown, she had detected hints that he wished to avoid contact with Santa Claus. Whatever his reasons, it was best to keep her return simple.

Wendy sat back in her sleigh, took the reins, and shouted, "Okay, Galatea my love, take us home."

Venga watched as Adrasteia stared northward.

"Pan's stepdaughter has landed," said the Tooth Fairy. "She's busy scattering her daydreams all over their picture-perfect, Christmas-card winterscape. Fool girl isn't paying attention. So up we go."

Gronk led the way, Venga close behind. The Tooth Fairy brought up the rear, keeping a far eye always on Wendy at the North Pole and urging them on. "Faster, you lazy laggards. Pick up the pace, damn you."

Annoying little bitch!

Venga hated flying in Gronk's wake. He stank like week-old road kill. But damned if he didn't know Wendy's route in minute detail.

They sped through the task, Venga's hand twisting to the right in a near rote flurry. But she took the time to savor the damage inflicted on each under-psyche, imagining that such savorings gave a unique spin to each series of wounds she delivered.

The Tooth Fairy really went manic in the bedroom of a child named Ginny Mae Falco. Sunlight streamed through the window and the bedroom's occupant was at school. The venom in Adrasteia's words spewed in all directions. She blasted the child's bed, the frilly-shaded lamp, and the cartoonish nightlight, vowing to drench Ginny Mae's bedroom in blood on the day the psyche switch occurred.

"Calm down," Venga said.

"Fuck if I will," replied the Tooth Fairy. "There's no time to waste. Off with you!"

And they resumed their breakneck pace.

The only time Venga paused—man, did the Tooth Fairy give her holy hell—was at their first jet full of doomed passengers. Why bother with their psyches? But miracles happened all the time. It would not do to leave even one mortal alive with a perfected psyche.

So she sped along the ranks of psyches awaiting the buckled-in bodies and sabotaged them all.

Nothing to chance.

At Venga's final flurry of wrist turns, the Tooth Fairy gave one last scan—yes, Wendy was still in the dark—and hustled them back to her island.

As the Tooth Fairy raced home, she bristled with orgasmic energy. Venga angered her and turned her on. As always, rage and lust played well together.

She led Venga and Gronk to the shore where the Easter Bunny had dropped thirteen huge chocolate eggs, their stench of divinity having been shat upon with gold that, instead of smashing them, had melted mid-air and gold-leafed them in a protective coating.

Now a heightened resolve drove her to dive-bomb the eggs. Above them she flew, Venga close behind.

She pulled up and glared at Gronk.

"Buzz off, junior, or I'll wrench your goddamn head off."

Without a word, he sped away.

Hesitation.

She had tried dive-bombing these eggs before and never quite touched them. They had that same kind of spell as the bedrooms of rug rats, a spell that drained the energy from her rage as she approached them.

She grabbed Venga in a lover's death grip, pinning her arms against her sides.

"What the—?"

Then she pressed her lips against Venga's.

There followed a magnificent, bloody, rough-and-tumble bout of sexual frenzy. They tossed and turned in midair, fisting hanks of hair, scoring skin and gold metallic covering, biting down hard everywhere, and letting blood and ichor. As they sped toward mutual climax, the Tooth Fairy aimed their bodies at the eggs and down they went.

Their orgasmic energy redoubled.

They picked up speed.

Down they hurtled in a whoosh of ecstasy. This time, damage to the eggs was inevitable. In their first sweep and spiral of climax, they sheared away the tops of the eggs. In ever-speedier spiralings, off came sections of chocolate egg, gilt spangling free in golden shavings.

Thus they reclaimed that long forbidden shore, reveling in the ruin about to overwhelm the human race.

Somewhere in there, Quint had shown up and now watched the frenzy of their fuck, intent his gaze, his eyes burrowing deep into them.

CHAPTER NINETEEN
THE SEVEN BILLION FUCKS
OF NICHOLAS THE SAINT

How sweet of Gregor, Wendy thought, to invite her over for a private tea party with his new friend Gaven, one of Hephaestus's golden girls. After the community of elves had welcomed her home, full of laughter and glee, a few quiet hours were just what she needed.

Through the gathering dusk, she walked from her gingerbread house to the stables. Gregor stood as he often did at the doorway, peering out over the half-door. But instead of his eternal scowl, he wore a look that defied description. Part watchfulness it was, part eagerness, the rest a swirl of unreadable emotions.

Leave it to Gregor to shun the female elves in favor of a golden girl. No other golden girl had, to Wendy's knowledge, ventured out of the psyche factory. But Gaven was different, just the sort an outsider like Gregor would take up with.

"Welcome, my dear." He gave her a perfunctory hug that said, *On the whole, I'd rather not touch you—but one does what one must.*

"Thank you, Gregor. This is so kind of you."

Just inside the door stood Gaven, her gold-coated pupils impossible to read. Yet there radiated from the sun-yellow sheen of her skin a natural warmth.

"Ah, if it isn't humanity's great deliverer!"

Gaven's voice had a flakey, lemony richness. The light from Gregor's lantern flared across her lips as she spoke, making it seem as though her syllables peeled off and scalloped through the air.

"Pleased to meet you," said Wendy, extending her hand. Gaven grasped it just a teensy bit too long and too firm.

"The water's set to boil, Wendy," said Gregor. "Your choice of tea sits on the table."

"I've never known you to drink tea," she said with some astonishment.

He laughed. "One of many vices Gaven here has introduced me to. Sit, dear girl, sit. Tell us all about how you seeded the globe with goodness."

And so she did, answering their intent looks with a narrative that lasted well into the evening.

Finally, she begged off extending her visit further. But she pleaded with him—and he granted her wish—to peek in at the slumbering reindeer, whispering her love to each in turn and blowing them soft kisses. She saved for last the exhausted Galatea, her diminutive white-furred reindeer.

Gregor repeated his peculiar hug at the door with all the awkwardness of an inept dance partner.

Gaven contented herself with a wave and a nod of her head. Friendly or cold? Wendy could not tell.

Time for sleep, she thought, stifling a yawn. First thing tomorrow morning, I'll check on the state of affairs.

And oh, dear reader, check she did.

In disbelief, Wendy scanned tens of thousands of psyches awaiting insertion the world over.

What she saw brought on a rush of panic, a hot flush up the back of her neck swirling across her cheeks and forehead, pounding sweat and fear there.

"Something's wrong. Their psyches are worse than ever. The rush to destruction will be quicker than we had thought."

"Show me," said her stepfather.

Wendy projected Frank Worthington's future. Not simply wounding words awaited his wife, but fists as well. And the words he would use were vicious in the extreme, cutting deep into Krista Worthington, diminishing her, closing her down in ways impossible to reverse.

Jacques LaFramboise would quite go off his nut, tie up and gag his wife and daughter, then throttle them to death before overdosing on sleeping pills.

Willard Frist would talk his friends and employees into buying stock in his company, driving up the price. He would then sell all his shares and disappear. When the remaining shares became worthless, some of his CEO buddies would hire a hit man to find him.

As for Gillian Barnes, she was fated to stare into her empty life, spiral down into despair, go swiftly toward drugs and an overdose, leaving a suicide note so full of gloom and heartache that it took scores of readers down into a personal hell of their own.

Then Wendy brought multitudes of ruined psyches before Santa's eyes, laying out the venality destined to wound or destroy lives. The rosy hue had long drained from his cheeks. "Are they all like that?"

She began to say yes, but tears overwhelmed her.

Santa gathered her in his arms.

"There, there, dear," he said. Then, "We're going to need help. Lots of it."

He knelt, Wendy beside him, and begged for divine intervention.

At once Michael appeared.

Beside him stood the Son, who spirited them in the blink of an eye to the psyche factory.

The Easter Bunny, looking dazed, had clearly been snatched from his burrow and rushed here.

At the Son's request, Hephaestus and his golden handmaidens suspended operations.

Santa peered deeply into the psyche that had been set before him, quickly noting the means by which his re-engineering had been subverted. "Someone—and I think I know who—has been up to no good," he said. "The connections between upper- and under-psyche have been thoroughly compromised."

The Son took over: "The problem lies not with your fixes, Santa Claus, but with a weakening of the sinews between upper and lower. If we could somehow coat them with love—"

Santa despaired. "Over seven billion psyches repaired before the tipping point? How could we hope to do that? Even if we had the means, magic time surely cannot be stretched that far."

"I can think of a way," said Aphrodite, a gleam in her eye.

She took the Son aside and spoke softly to him, smiling at his reply.

They rejoined the group.

Said the Son, "Certain improvements will be made to the originals here in the psyche factory. Wendy and I will head out to supervise the replacement of the compromised psyche with one strengthened by love. The Easter Bunny will track our route from here, pulling out the next psyche slated for repair and replacement."

Santa looked puzzled. "What repairs are possible at this point? And how are they to be realized in time to avert disaster?"

"That's where you come in, Santa," replied the Son. "You and the Goddess of Love."

Aphrodite's smile was decidedly impish.

"The Easter Bunny is to set the psyche before you both, at which time you and she are to make love in such magnitude and with such fervor—matching your erotic zeal to the unique soul set before you—that your love bathes the upper-psyche deep and wide.

"At the Easter Bunny's signal, I will overlay the new original with the one before me."

Santa gaped, goggled, and forgot to breathe. His cheeks were flushed with excitement and disbelief.

"It's that simple? But what about magic time?"

The Son assured, "This calls for a special exception, and a special exception shall be made."

"I'll need my wives' permission. And Hephaestus, do we have *your* permission?"

The blacksmith snorted. "Of course. My wife is nothing if not over-the-top insatiable. Maybe being fucked billions of times will cool her ardor, let me get some rest for a change."

"Ah," said Santa. "Wendy, please ask your—"

But even as he spoke, his wives had been swept in, so urgent was the divine summons.

Santa explained it all to them.

"Of course it's all right," said Rachel.

And Anya agreed. "Humankind must be saved at all costs.

But darling," she said, "do you think you're up to it?"

As she spoke, Santa could not tear his gaze away from Aphrodite, such was her beauty, such his joy at the thought of the divine coupling that would soon connect them so many times with such variety and so deeply.

"We shall see."

His calm surprised him.

And so it came to pass.

Dear reader, language fails even to begin to convey the wonders of their coupling, this Aphrodite in all her changeable forms and the fine intermingling of Santa and Pan which rose to embrace the Goddess of Love's next incarnation, engaging her in the most pure, most angelic, most animalistic love and exploding into the sweetest cunt in all creation the ecstasy of his fluidic love. Each time they climaxed, a love-mist rose from them to drift over and descend on the psyche by the Easter Bunny's side.

His wild, wondering eyes blessed them as he stood there, efficient in his assigned tasks even as his back feet came near to thumping her bower's packed earth in erotic sympathy.

Each newly anointed psyche was swept away as he tapped it to signal the Son. Then in a flicker, he sped to the archives to pull out the next psyche on Wendy's path. The ones he sent on their way had a faint blue tinge to them—so there would be no doubt, when they arrived, that the compromised psyche had been shored up by immortal love.

As Santa moved toward Aphrodite for the first time, she said to him, "You must fuck me with every part of your being. Hold nothing back. Judge no part of you unworthy. All is perfect, even those parts you've been tempted to condemn so harshly."

And so he serviced her, becoming over those seven billion couplings far more than the superb lover he had always been. Setting all sides of him free to come forth into the world of love, he became the greatest, most caring lover the world had ever known, the male epitome of a tumescence most sensitive to his lover's quicksilver needs.

After all of this was over, Rachel and Anya thrilled to the change in their husband and opened even more to the power of Eros inside them.

As Wendy and the Savior dashed across the globe, countering the damage the Tooth Fairy had intended, theirs was a similar though non-sexual connection.

Gradually there grew in the heavens above them—following them as a rainbow persists in a traveler's eye—an image of the Son nailed naked to the cross. With each healed psyche, the face of the crucified Christ reflected an infinitesimal increase of pain and of pleasure.

"Will you be all right?" asked Wendy.

"Always."

And she turned, satisfied, to the next psyche.

Wild gyrations spun in the Easter Bunny's brain.

He had been a voyeur from as far back as memory went. Generative acts—the aromas, the fluids, the unclothed flesh, the screams and sighs of bliss—had always excited him.

For one thing, they accentuated his loneliness and thereby sharpened his self-definition.

For another, he enjoyed the frequent mind arousal that came with doing what should not be done. The fuck-drenched mortals dancing so sweetly before him thought themselves unseen in their intimacies. That thrilled him, gave him power over them, and made his loneliness more bearable.

But above all, nothing in all of the Father's creation was more beautiful that two creatures engaged an act of copulation. And there was really no better vantage point than his—within easy reach of them, within eye-sight and nose-whiff, his ears enflamed blush-red by the sounds of mouth, loin, and lip.

Now here he stood, boldly mind-erect (for reasons that escaped him, he sported no genitalia), witness to the greatest acts of copulation that would ever be—between the goat god rampant and the goddess who embodied erotic impulse in its most beautiful female forms.

They transformed his feelings about voyeurism. No longer did he call it that. No, this was witnessing. This was being a blessed observer.

True, they knew he was there.

But they paid no attention to him nor did they mind his presence. That was quite clear.

Soon, the creepy aspects of bearing witness to the fuck-and-suck of living beings withered away, to be replaced by a magnificent grace.

The energy of full orgasm without climax filled his body, soul, and spirit. There was no need of anything else, nothing but a soft intense light surrounding and embracing his being.

Even as the immortal couple irradiated each psyche brought before them with love, so too did his psyche feel that irradiation.

There was one other change.

He had done his best to suppress all memory of the rapes he had committed in past years, against human females yes but especially against Rachel, Santa's wife once mortal and Wendy's mother.

Now those acts came starkly into prominence.

They were unforgivable, not that he had ever tried forgiving himself for them.

There they were, arrayed before him, even as he did his part to save humankind.

And there they stayed.

Sometimes, the awfulness of one's past became an unwelcome guest, lurking or lazing in a dark corner. Now it sat there, not invisible, not trying to dress itself in appealing garb nor demanding attention.

"Welcome," he told it. "I wish I had never brought you into existence. But I did. Here you are. And here I'll welcome you all the days of my life. You are part of me. Sit easily. Ask nothing. I will feed you only what you need.

"Above all, though judgment I deserve and harsh, I will not judge myself. Nor will I judge others."

That made him feel . . . not better, exactly, but as good as possible under the circumstances.

He shot his glance across the earth, cheered by the steady advance of the faint blue light that meant love-basted psyches lay in waiting.

***

Although she could not have foreseen the benefits that would redound upon her as the more than seven billion fucks neared their conclusion, Wendy followed through on a powerful hunch.

First she confirmed her suspicions with the Son, who swiftly summoned the Easter Bunny.

His head spun. His ears flopped. "What? Why am I here, if I may be so bold?" Some damned somebody's bedroom, vacant but for these beloved immortals and now himself, abruptly snatched from the Goddess of Love's bower.

"Later," said Wendy. "For now, please just do what we ask."

It sounded pretty damned weird to him and not a little scary, but he agreed and winked back into the psyche factory, summoning his favorite golden girl and issuing a command. Right after the final human psyche had been patched up and sent forth into the world, she was to bring him the psyche of God the Father Himself.

To his astonishment, it was scarcely larger than the largest human psyche.

"Why has this—?" began Santa, lying in bliss beside Aphrodite and clearly savoring what he thought had been their last climax.

"It's Wendy's idea," said the Easter Bunny. "With the Son's backing, I hasten to add. Trust them, Santa. Fuck first, ask questions later."

Inspired by the presence of that Most Divine of All Psyches, the love that Santa and Aphrodite then made exceeded in sensitivity, caring, and kindness anything that had gone before. And the misty blue veil of love that lay upon and sank into God's psyche carried more healing power than any that had preceded it.

But it's what the Easter Bunny did at the moment of shared climax that made all the difference to Wendy.

He gave his nose an extra special twitch.

And born, upon the instant, to the pair engaged in their

divine explosion was a young god, aged nine, at once given the name Adonis, so handsome and full of life was he.

What impact that birth had upon Wendy we shall see very shortly. As also the effects of the change on the Father God Himself.

Patience, dear reader, patience.

CHAPTER TWENTY
AWAKENINGS MORTAL
AND IMMORTAL

All of this flew under the Tooth Fairy's radar.

So hungry was she to feast on the bones of Ginny Mae Falco that she tracked only that sleeping child's gentle breathing. The love-reinforced psyche waiting nearby escaped her notice.

Once she had passed through Ginny Mae's bedroom door, her bloodlust was as usual muted. She hunkered down dead center on the carpet.

Would those damned do-gooders, Wendy and the Son, notice her there when they zipped in to swap out the child's psyche?

Fuck if she cared. It would all happen so fast, in the thousandth flicker of an eyelid, it wouldn't even occur to them to wonder at her presence.

Then the moment happened.

The waiting psyche had vanished from where it had hovered, settling into place inside the girl.

Endgame.

And the beginning of the end.

The Tooth Fairy sucked in a breath, high on savoring her coming triumph, anticipating how sweet would be the taste of the child's bones.

Dread.

But how could—?

That she had failed—and failed grandly—came upon her with a terrible certainty. The bloodlust she longed to bathe in simply failed to manifest. When she scanned the sleeping child's body, she was struck dumb.

She stood and fumblefooted backward through the door and into the hallway. There her rage upswelled. Above the modest house she rose. Her head whipped this way and that, surveying the world entire.

She had been bested again.

And for that, someone would pay.

Back to her island she sped. From every part of the globe, soundless shouts of jubilation filled the air. She shot a glance at the North Pole and saw the creatures who had once been nymphs and satyrs marveling at the same sight that touched off firestorms of fury in her.

Indeed, Santa and Wendy, Michael and the Son, and all those that kept company with them, peered deep into the new human psyches and their hearts took flight.

Scales had fallen from mortal eyes.

Take Ginny Mae, for example.

In good little boys and girls, the changes were less apparent than in grown-ups. But Wendy directed Santa's gaze inward to the softness, the gentleness, the wide and free new stance toward all things that Ginny, rubbing her eyes awake, took.

Then Santa and his stepdaughter broadened their view to encompass the entire human race.

In time, they would witness the changes in action, moment by moment. For now, the mass of humanity took on a suggestive hue.

Mortals blinked and looked about.

Not a word was spoken, not a step taken.

Then the transformed ones started to speak and move and grow.

And the new dance began.

You may be wondering what impact all of this had on God the Father? It might well be supposed that the resentment steadily building in Him toward Saint Nick would eventually erupt, to no good end.

After all, it was He Who had brought the serpent to the Tooth Fairy's island. And it was He Who had given Quint the power to summon Venga from Hades' arms. God had set the psyche factory both in heaven and at the North Pole so that Venga could sneak in and steal psyches. And He had chosen to answer Santa's prayer for help, with females who had once been fuckable and frequently fucked tree nymphs, distractions then to Santa and his male elves.

What terrible acts might this major chance provoke in such a god as this?

But the Father's refurbished psyche, marinated in Santa and Aphrodite's redemptive love, put paid to any hint of creator's hubris, erased all envy of Santa's fixes to the Father's botched work, and softened Him toward a new strength and assurance.

The immediate effect was the Shame Son's fade to black. That mealy-mouthed whisperer in his father's ear simply slunk away unnoticed, no last words, never to return.

The first thing the Father did then was to reach out and bring Wendy and Adonis before His throne.

"Okay, you two. Here's your cottage at the North Pole." He waved His right hand and up it popped in the woods, fully formed and functional, white smoke skirling up from its chimney. "In default, each of you has the body, though not the mind, of a nine-year-old."

Wendy said, "Dear Lord, I've always wanted—"

"And you shall have it. You can experiment with any age between nine and a hundred and nine. For your first make-out, I suggest twenty-two for you, Adonis, and thirty-five for Wendy. Whenever either of you dips below the age of consent, the sexual urge will drop to zero in both. Questions?"

"No, sir."

"No, sir."

The glances they gave one another answered every possible question.

The Father set them in their cottage and left them to get acquainted. Foreseeing how that would go, He pronounced it very good indeed.

Next, He turned to the elves.

Male and female analyzed He them, delving into their need for companionship, examining degrees of sexual perversity, working out ideal couplings and ways to maximize their delight while minimizing the distractibility factor in Santa's workshop.

138

He then further enhanced the huts, hovels, and cottages he had once created for the female elves. Above the door of each dwelling He inscribed the name of a female elf. According to the complex of desires He had found in some of the elves, He worked out agendas for stable connections. In other cases, He devised rotating rosters of sexual pairings.

Henceforth, there was never any contention about such matters. Reliable as clockwork, the males knew precisely which cottage to head for at the close of the workday. Their belongings had already been moved to that predestined hut, as had their favorite dishes and cookware and the foodstuffs they required from pantry or fridge.

What then became of the dormitory?

That turned into a way station, ideal for naps, for gussying up in the communal bathroom, or for quick rolls in the hay—rare, those. The bunk beds were kept spotless, but were never thereafter used, except for the occasional, spur-of-the-moment love-tumble.

Now, He thought, for a certain purveyor of colored eggs and jelly beans, hunkered down in a vast burrow overseeing the manufacture of candy and baskets.

His sudden appearance startled the creature.

"Stand tall, you furry fucker. I have work to do!"

"Yes, God, sir."

The Easter Bunny's already active imagination the Father God vividified to the max. His stupidly bright face beamed a gazillion times brighter. Not once thrown by the shift in him, the Easter Bunny accepted the illusion—fully realized—of his mate Petunia now enfleshed and scores of tiny kid bunnies hopping all about. The little ones frolicked. Petunia fucked him and kept him company in every other way. Why, he even began bringing her along on his voyeuristic adventures.

All of it, an internal masturbatory monologue.

He never knew the difference and became, as a result, a better Easter Bunny.

Weep not for him, gentle reader, for his life was grand. Oh, there was one tiny flaw which we will get to in due course.

Last on the Father's to-do list was the Tooth Fairy.

139

And do her he did.

Venga too.

As for Quint, God simply wiped the slimy imp out.

Said He, "Into oblivion with you!"

And Quint was duly obliviated.

Venga He gave to Gregor. Enough shilly-shallying about them. Well might one dread putting those two together, fearing havoc. Not so. For Venga kept all her simmering inside, never tempted to share it with anyone. She still fascinated but in a sour, frozen way. Her golden skin shone as if it were dipped in vinegar.

And Gregor?

Well, whenever Gregor was tempted to give voice to his scowls, or reveal what Anya and the elves had done to get back at her philandering husband, all that came from his lips were blessings most inventive and generous. And when he stopped trying to say it and tried writing it down instead, the paper turned into a Christmas card that brought tears of joy to anyone who read it.

The Tooth Fairy had it worst of all.

In mid-rant against her sons, the Father God took her by the throat and brought her to the heights of the mountain on her island. There He forced her to her knees, her buttocks upthrust, her legs spread wide, her nose and one cheek pressed against cold stone.

In that position, He enchained her, her wrists and ankles held in harsh granite cuffs.

"Damn you, Zeus," she shouted, "you sorry excuse for a creator. Unshackle me!"

"Fat chance."

A Quint-like automaton He set behind her, turning the imp into a well-oiled, stone-cold mechanism of anal rape, relentlessly violating.

Its hips thrust. Streams of thin coins shot up inside her without cease. The thing's cock was chilled, rough, and abrasive. She had no way to convert the coins to bone, no way to puke them out. They bloated her gut with blockages of solid gold.

Every evening, God cloned her in that state and sent the clone out to love children, dine on teeth, and eke out coins from her anus until she grew slim once more and the chained fairy on the mountain top unbloated in sympathy with her, only to be rebloated when the night deliveries were done. The Tooth Fairy protested, not letting up for one moment. Cowering on the beach, her imps covered their ears against their mother's screams.

In the hours following the grand switcheroo, Santa and Wendy scrutinized humankind intently.

Beneath the excited hum and buzz of the mortals now awake, they tasted a delicious mix of creativity, confidence, and lightheartedness. An electromagnetic realigning toward sanity had happened on a global scale. Gone were base—and baseless—assumptions. Gone too all retreats into judgment that erected and thickened barriers between people.

No need for grand declarations of intent: There was a sudden end to war, shared horror at how counter to humanity war had always run, and swift reconciliation between those who had once been enemies. Indeed, the word "enemy" lost its meaning and dropped from everyone's lexicon.

No longer were police or security forces of any kind needed. Soldiers lay down their weapons, shucked off their uniforms, and returned to civilian life.

Eyes that had been hooded in despair were opened to possibility. Minds that had too easily made a home for fear now embraced new directions and pressed on with confidence toward common goals.

The changes Santa and Wendy observed ran the gamut from subtle to dramatic.

Tracey Fineman from Longmont, Colorado, halfway through reciting a long list of a friend's shortcomings, turned mid-sentence on a dime. In her mind, that list morphed into a litany of her friend's virtues. Without missing a beat, her peroration turned into a garden of praise and a suggestion—at once heeded—that she call her friend and tell her so.

Halfway across the world, Dieter Schultz in Linz, Austria

eased his finger off the trigger of his pistol, put on the safety, and said to his wife, "Wow, sorry, sweets. I have no idea what *that* was all about. Let's chuck this awful thing." To which she, pleased at her refusal to blame him for anything, said, "Dieter, you're a good man beneath all the shit, which thankfully God has suddenly lifted from you. Let's proceed." Together they turned from a past they no longer felt the need to examine, toward a future now being born.

And clinical psychologist Dora Medgyesy in Wells, England watched Thomas Trent, a thoroughly fucked up and potentially suicidal client turn into a mentally healthy, unflinching, and courageous man from one eyeblink to the next.

At the North Pole, the seismic shift in human behavior led to several radical changes.

On the distaff side, though Santa didn't see it that way—more like joyously bad news—the Naughty List, for the first time in forever, was blessedly empty. More toys would be required. Overnight, Santa planned and built an extension to the workshop, giving thanks that the female elves had doubled his workforce. Still, their Christmas deadline would be tight this year.

There was plenty of unequivocally good news.

No need ever again to deliver lumps of coal. That would benefit the planet.

Humankind's spirited embrace of Zero Population Growth—gone the entrenched insanity of resistance to birth control—would lead to a dramatic tapering off of newborns and hence of young children. At last, there would be a brake on impulsive breeding and so too a cap on the number of little boys and girls Santa would need to visit every Christmas.

And Wendy would see an exponential explosion in the number of children with gifted futures. At once, she increased her annual Christmas Eve visits from a hundred to ten thousand.

"Astonishing, isn't it," said Santa, "how, second by second, the whole tenor of humankind is changing? It's like a single organism reorienting itself, pointing to true north at last."

Wendy tried to speak but words failed her.

Santa had to content himself—and highly content he proved to be—with the warmest embrace she had ever given him.

CHAPTER TWENTY-ONE
HOW EVERYTHING WENT
ALL AJUMBLE AGAIN

Two weeks went by in utter bliss.

The swift, multifaceted recognition of the oneness of all humankind galloped on apace. Stewards of the earth all men and women became.

Television was threatened with instant extinction, so little interest did it hold for the engaged human mind. Film projects not yet wrapped were shelved as curios of a time past, even as a flowering of new film ideas augured exceptionally well for future flick fun.

Venal, easily bought, and power-hungry politicians underwent instant transformations into statesmen of the highest caliber. Some at once resigned, knowing themselves incapable of such a transformation, taking up trades more suited to their temperaments, such as butcher, pest control officer, and dog walker.

In all areas of planning—and in the revision of old plans gone awry—there were at last prized and put to work highly intelligent people versed in whatever area they were drawn to, not penned in by ways that had gone before, eager to experiment with bold new risks yet not falling foolhardily into fads, not even enslaved to their own ideas should they prove faulty.

Things were moving exceptionally well and with blinding speed.

Until, that is, the Almighty changed His mind.

God looked down from above with pure love, no longer eaten with envy as He observed the patched psyches in operation, amazed and delighted at the new directions the human race was taking.

"This is the sort of thing I had in mind all along," said He to no one in particular.

In the divinity that was His mind, He brought back the old psyches, the role of free will in them, and the weaknesses that had made good choices difficult. And He saw that His former methods, the human psyches as He had initially made them, were in some strange way exceptionally good.

"Oh come now, really?" He asked Himself.

And Himself replied, "Why, yes, these little buggers have real merit. They're not a botch at all, not a one of them. Tell You what. How about I compromise, just a little."

He gazed fondly upon them.

He loved them.

And with a sweep of His hand, He chose to restore the under-psyches, leaving intact the love-anointed over-psyches, remembering as well to buffer the reversion so that men and women would not go mad as this latest change hit them.

The elves who worked in the psyche factory were not so buffered. They felt a massive tremor in their inventory and in the psyches they were toying with at that moment. Santa, immediately summoned by them and bringing Wendy with him, felt a surge of panic as he surveyed the world.

He asked Hephaestus the obvious question.

The blacksmith simply nodded. "The under-psyches have all changed back to what they were. Both here and in the archives."

Santa and Wendy exchanged worried looks.

"How could such a thing have happened?" asked Santa.

"Only by a sweep of the Father's hand, I suspect," replied the blacksmith. And as an afterthought, "We have backups of everything we've done, in case God ever changes His mind or someone persuades Him to do so."

As soon as those words were spoken, the Son stood before them. "I'll check," he said. Swiftly gone and come back, he confirmed that it had been the Father's doing, all right, and that it had been done not out of spite but love.

Santa sighed. "What do we do now?"

And the Son, with a smile that warmed the hearts of everyone present, said, "Oh ye of little faith. Look on and marvel!"

145

***

I would be remiss if I failed to observe that Santa Claus had undergone profound changes during his bout of marathon lovemaking with the Goddess of Love.

Aphrodite had opened up to him in so many ways that he no longer felt the least shame or suppression regarding his Pan persona. He had taken her—and she him—with joy and compassion, with brutish lust and generosity, with grace, fire, and ice. His climaxes rang out with a joyful noise, with magnificent gushing geysers of explosive love that brought the full range of his lung power into play.

If for no other reason than that, Anya and Rachel were abundantly grateful that they had granted their husband his seven billion fucks. For his erotic skills, already at a peak, peaked higher still.

Aphrodite had taught him unbounded love, and his complete and generous embrace of his wives gifted them with that same unbounded love.

But a far more important change had come over the jolly old elf.

His opinion of the human race had always been mixed. He had favored nice children over naughty. He had blocked all adult misbehavior—there was so goddamned much of it— from his mind. But now that he had seen into each human psyche, observed its botched construction, forgiven its sinful ways, and doused it with generous outpourings of healing love, his heart had softened.

It could truly be said that Santa Claus deeply loved every human being on the planet, even before his and Aphrodite's entwined climaxes had bestowed the gift of a final fix to their over-psyches.

So it was not without a great deal of anxiety that Santa, standing beside Wendy in the psyche factory, observed the human race at this critical juncture, now that their under-psyches had reverted to God's botch.

Would they backslide into habitual misbehavior?

Would their amazing strides toward peace, love, and

understanding be reversed and forgotten?

Would war, greed, fear, tribalism, bigotry, blame, scapegoating, xenophobia, and all the rest of their tiresome failings once more rule the day?

It didn't take long to answer those questions.

Wendy's smile told the tale.

Santa's heart basked in the glow of that smile and in what he and his stepdaughter observed worldwide.

The taste of moral sanity and the sheer joy of human cooperation, combined with the overlay of love in the over-psyche, had been enough to tip the human race toward maintaining, sustaining, and developing their new modes of behavior further.

Despite the under-psyche's knee-jerk propensity toward greed, fear, and lust, their love-strengthened will to choose sane courses of action, both individually and in groups, proved far stronger.

John Milton had once described human beings as "sufficient to have stood, though free to fall." With the strengthening of the worthiest human tendencies, standing had become a far easier choice, and falling an extremely unlikely outcome.

"It looks as if they're going to make it," said Wendy.

"Indeed it does," said Santa, giving her a hug.

There was one other item on Santa's mind. During his joyous lovemaking with Aphrodite, several of her incarnations had reminded him of the Tooth Fairy, so passionate, so possessive, and so savage.

Compassion for his once secret lover filled Santa's heart.

What could he do for her? How might he soften the harshness of her fate? During their affair, despite his subsequent rejection of her, he had been quite fond of her. Strong women who knew what they wanted and went after it, guns blazing, turned him on.

He approached Aphrodite then, ran his plan by her, and got her nod of approval.

He would of course need the blessings of his wives, blessings not tepid but enthusiastic.

He sat with them in the living room.

First the three of them shared their joy at the turn of events on earth. The chatter was incessant and full of wonder.

Then he spoke up. "Dear Anya, my darling Rachel, I have a plan to reform the Tooth Fairy."

"But Claus," said Anya, looking askance, "hasn't she fought everything you've tried to do since you broke off your affair with her?"

Rachel added a long litany of her misdeeds, though she ended with: "Still, if you want to forgive her—"

"I do. My plan, though, involves going to her as Pan and bedding her with the same ferocity and passion I did way back when. Just once, I promise. And only if I have your permission, full on, without hesitation."

Rachel sat stunned.

"Give it some thought," he said.

Anya bluntly resisted. It was monstrous, she said. It was unnecessary. It would arouse expectations. And it might put his family in even worse jeopardy.

Santa then launched into his purest, most generous paean of love to them both, giving every assurance, offering from the depths of his heart his devotion to these two wonderful women. He coaxed and cajoled, not making light of the act he was intending, but not making over much of it either. He had been granted Aphrodite's blessing, he said, a thing not easily given. And the goddess had assured him that there would be no untoward repercussions, nothing ongoing, nothing set in motion for having roused the Tooth Fairy's lust.

And in the end, with Santa's assurances and promise of just-this-once, he won them over.

"I vow," he said, "to relate all that happens in detail. And to bring back the energy she and I generate and stoke the fires of our marriage with it, as I did with the lovemaking Aphrodite and I shared."

That perked them both up.

Indeed, they took that opportunity to vanish into magic time and savor their changed hubby for hours and days on end.

***

That night around the dinner table, with Anya's steaming apple strudel delighting them and Santa bursting forth with his usual gustatory orgasms in appreciation of Anya's cooking, Wendy raised a cautious hand.

"Uh oh," said Santa with a smile. "Whenever Wendy raises a cautious hand, trouble's a-brewing."

With a laugh, Wendy confided in Adonis, who sat fresh-faced on her left, "You'll get used to Santa's brand of humor soon enough."

"It's delightful," said Adonis. "But, please, dear, let us all know what's going on."

"I've found a teensy little problem," she said, "which will eventually grow much worse if we don't address it soon."

In the open space beside the hutch of dark cherry wood with its decorative plates and Hummel figures, Wendy projected an image of the large volume that contained two lists separated by a heavy red divider, one for the Naughty, one for the Nice.

"Watch the position of the divider as the future unfolds."

She sped up time.

Slow and steady, the size of the Naughty list grew from no entries to hundreds, thousands, then tens of thousands of names. The Nice list shrank in tandem.

Santa rose, alarmed. "How is that possible?"

"Stay calm, Daddy. Here's the problem. Newborns lack the love-charge you and Aphrodite added to the over-psyches of mortals currently living. So there's nothing—other than the example of their elders—to keep them from straying eventually into the patterns of misbehavior we've just eradicated.

"If we do nothing, at some point a New Darkness is sure to engulf the world of mortals."

Rachel raced to the obvious solution first and Anya concurred with her.

Santa sat and relaxed, loving his two amazing wives more than ever.

He especially loved Rachel's beguiling suggestion for the concluding gesture each week.

"Let me run this by Aphrodite."

And into magic time he winked, back before they knew he was gone. Hints of lipstick, a deep ruby red, played around the soft white hairs on the left side of his mouth.

"Count her in, with an enthusiastic yes. She's up for all of it, starting this Sunday evening. I summoned the Savior, wanting to be sure that divine approval would be ours. And indeed we have the Father's blessing."

So it was that when Sunday arrived—and every Sunday thereafter—Anya and Rachel joined him in Aphrodite's bower. To them was assigned the task of bringing the psyches of that week's newborns, one by one, to the bower for a drenching of love.

The whole process didn't take too long, there being a mere three and a half million newborns each week. The presence of his wives gave Santa an added thrill, he so loved being watched and cheered on by them.

And of course that first time, there was the added thrill of anticipating the foursome that would bless the final newborn's psyche. His wives climaxed often during that first observation, though actually touching and being touched by Aphrodite brought them over in sweetly intense ways they could never have imagined.

By design too, their simultaneous four-way climax produced a love-anointing so pure that the newborn before whose psyche they had produced it was fated to be a magnificently inventive and polymorphously perverse lover soon after he or she reached the age of consent.

And so a weekly tradition was born, Santa raring to go the following morning into a week of toy making unparalleled in energy and excitement.

CHAPTER TWENTY-TWO
CHANGES ON A GRAND SCALE

Santa and Wendy never tired of admiring the new paths humankind was striking out on and contrasting them with the old awful ways of straying and sinning, of grasping and shying away, of pressing on in wrong directions and shamelessly acting the hypocrite, the puffed-up blowfish, or the pious motherfucker.

Indeed, they began to set aside Tuesday evenings to sit in the front room of the gingerbread house, sharing a big bowl of freshly popped popcorn sprinkled with brewer's yeast while surveying the world together.

Early on, Adonis had decided to bow out. This, he thought, was a special time for father and daughter. Besides which, he benefitted—as did Wendy—from her catching him up on what they had witnessed, the two of them sitting in that front room sampling the projections Wendy brought up.

Sometimes they focused on individuals writing or speaking truth, or simply bending to beautiful tasks. No wounding words did Santa and Wendy ever again hear, except on stage or screen where human beings reenacted, through the magic of story, the strayward behaviors recently abandoned. Regrets had become a thing of the past, as had anticipatory cravings.

Political categories softened, tribalism going the way of the dodo bird.

The world became a place of sharing, all things in common. Respect for property held only through a new and sustained respect for other people.

And what was the basis for that respect? No one chose, any longer, to tear down another in order to build themselves up. Instead they shored up others, saw and encouraged only the beauty in those they met or broke bread with, forgave in the blink of an eye, expressed frequent gratitude, took no one for granted, and found frequent occasion for rejoicing in everyone they met.

Nothing calcified.

Identities were held lightly. So too any clinging to larger units of humanity. Organizations either found ways to serve the greater good or dissolved without regret. They had no time for regret and no time was devoted to it.

Santa said, "You know what I love most about it?"

"No," said Wendy.

Santa looked quizzical, bellied up a great guffaw, and confided, "Me neither. Why assign rankings? I love that all of their wasteful bickering has stopped. That they're now genuine stewards of their planet, letting the insights of the wisest thinkers lead them toward its healing. That they no longer act out of scarcity, but abundance. And most of all, I love their newfound respect for creativity and play.

"As for violence? They simply don't go there. Not in any serious way. In games, yes. But games remain just that, things of filigree and joy. They no longer treat them as matters of life and death, getting in the way of mutual respect."

They checked in on Jacques and Dominique LaFramboise. That couple, who had previously seemed so dead to one another, now went about gazing into each other's eyes and breaking into joyous laughter. There was talk of adopting a child, of honoring each the other's independence, of giving serious time to cultivating friendships new and old.

Willard Frist, the CEO from hell, had completely reversed himself and was arranging a generous buyout so his employees could own the company. He had also slashed his ridiculously high salary to a quarter of what it had been, with a promise to lower it further as he introduced austerity into his spending.

And Gillian Barnes had dismounted from her high horse and sent it, with a smart flank-slap, galloping off to places unknown. She had already noted and reined in her tendency to regard herself as superior to others. Such nonsense, a way of living that flung up barriers to the intimacy she had hitherto lacked in her life.

"I love how she's mellowed yet not surrendered any of her strength," said Wendy.

"And look," said Santa. "Do you see how her friends and loved ones have changed in response?" They had begun, these friends, to stand closer to her, to give her welcome embraces. The unbridgeable gaps and high walls that had once existed had simply vanished.

"Amazing," said Wendy.

Then Santa excitedly: "Bring up the Worthingtons!"

And so she did.

There sat Frank and Krista in a park near their home. Their faces were softer than Santa had ever seen them and their eyes connected beyond the need for words.

Yet words there were.

"I feel as if I'm seeing you for the first time," said Frank, his eyes moist. "You're so precious to me, dear Krista, such a beautiful gift. I can see the little girl in you and the grown woman, both adorable."

And she said, "It feels good to be appreciated. You had become hard over the years, but now you're soft and embracing. I like the change."

Boy, did she ever. The depth of that liking sounded in her words, and Santa and his stepdaughter reveled in them.

When they were done looking at Frank and Krista Worthington, Wendy brought out a surprise, hiding behind a stack of books in her bookshelves. It was Santa's long-ago list of the shortcomings of adult mortals. Together by lamplight they went over the tens of thousands of egregious faults and saw that every one of them had been eradicated. No matter how thoroughly they scoured the earth, not a single counter-instance could they come up with.

"Well," said Santa sitting back. "I'd say this calls for a hot toddy. Do you agree?"

And agree she did.

There were new adjustments at the North Pole.

Back when the Father had sprouted cozy little huts in the woods for the female elves, Gregor had been left out of the pairings-up. He had no mate and was clearly uninterested in having one. So he continued to live at the stables, grumped

153

down into a frown that deepened day by day. He only endured being sexual with Venga on her occasional visits.

But on the day of humanity's transformation, a new hut sprang up in the same general area of the woods, distant from the rest and pretty much out of earshot.

A small shed adjoined the hut. It held a generous supply of paint cans, paint trays, rollers, and brushes. The paint color matched the interior walls of the hut, an off-white tinged with a hint of egg-shell blue.

One moment, Gregor sat at his desk in the stables. The next, he was standing before the hut, Venga at his side. Ninety seconds before, Santa had said to Rachel and Anya, "I don't care what Gregor and Venga do, as long as they don't do it in the stables and frighten the reindeer." The Father, having pondered those words in His heart, waved the hut into existence.

Now the grumpiest elf stared into the shed. "Hmm, I wonder what all that paint is for."

"Damned if I know," said Venga.

But when they entered the hut, all became clear.

For at the sight of the bed, they fell into a frenzy of lust—wild beasts clawing at clothing, flesh, and metal. Gregor's blood flowed and gushed. When he savaged Venga, golden ichor ran down her thighs.

Splashes red and gold flew hither and yon, turning the walls, ceiling, and floor into thick-flung murals of Pollack-like madness.

With this bestial tearing came bellows and screams pitched so high that forest life fled for miles around and elves relaxing or making love in their huts raised up on one elbow to tease out terrifying soundscapes from the air and wonder what that faint disturbance might mean.

They soon understood.

One day, Herbert had headed out for a walk, his camera about his neck. Near Gregor's hut, he had chanced upon a snowy clearing bathed in brilliant splashes of red and gold. He clicked and snapped, wondering what its origins were. Later, he turned those photos into an artistic study.

But while he was capturing the landscape from as many angles as possible, there came the sounds of rough sex from Gregor's hut. Herbert had crept up and peered cautiously in at the window as hot liquid went flying inside, spattering the window glass and wrapping the air in spiraling ribbons of blood and ichor. Gregor hunched bizarrely naked, his lumpy buttocks painted in gore. The burnished gold from Venga's mouth sparkled upon the rushing rapids of her screams.

Herbert withdrew, his ears ringing with the bellows and booms, his eyes burning from an assault of violent intercourse.

He confided only in Fritz, who brought it to Santa's ears and no further.

For a time, Santa feared this ferocious couple and the plots they might be hatching. Gregor, he knew, had never given up ideas of toppling him and taking charge.

Santa sent Fritz to eavesdrop.

Fritz reported back that in between bouts of sexual savagery, they plotted and schemed. But nothing ever came of their plans. Gregor and Venga soon proved to be an ineffectual Lord and Lady Macbeth and Santa knew he had nothing to fear from them, that he could find a sad sort of amusement in their inept dreams of usurpation.

Whenever he visited the stables, he humored them. The reindeer, as always, were safe with Gregor. He even had Fritz deliver gifts to the pair. Fritz reported how they had received the gifts, how they had put on pleasant faces—peculiar indeed when Gregor did it—and pretended to welcome him, all the while sending the clearest possible signals that they wanted him to leave as quickly as possible.

Gregor and Venga found a strange sort of comfort in one another, bitching and moaning incessantly, yet never wondering at their impotence when it came to following through. Bitter bickering set down roots in their relationship. Layered on top were digs and cuts at other North Polar residents. Tossing a vicious word salad kept their minds and tongues sharp.

So they passed their days in a mix of harshness and woe that sustained them and made them whole.

CHAPTER TWENTY-THREE
FURTHER CHANGES
ON A GRAND SCALE

As for the Tooth Fairy, Santa had first to free her from the eternal torment of being anally raped by the Quint thing. This he did—after consulting with the Son—by bringing the Tooth Fairy's psyche before the Goddess of Love and suggesting that they model their lovemaking after what she was enduring.

Santa slathered his cock with generous amounts of thick and viscous lubricant. Easing past the puckered muscle that ringed Aphrodite's anus and moving into the welcoming heat of her rectum, he reached around her right hip and fingered her clit to climax.

The energy of their love infused the psyche before them. Santa cleaned up, suited up, and reindeered up to deliver the altered psyche.

Below him, the Tooth Fairy's island shown rude and gash-like in the sea.

As his sleigh approached the mountaintop, he saw the Quint-shaped thing soften. It deflated and fell off its victim, dematerialized, and was gone in an instant.

The Tooth Fairy's granite shackles crumbled to dust.

Her gut mercifully debulked itself and rendered her svelte once more.

She lay there spent.

When she looked up, madness shone in her eyes. "Fuck me," she said in a whisper.

When Santa had stripped off his suit, standing before her was none other than Pan, the goat god with the raging hard-on, the horns, the stamping hooves, hair as harsh as steel wool everywhere on his body, and the sharp aromas of musk and love juice.

She lunged at him, wrenched his beast-jaws apart, and bit down on his back lower right molar, pulling it out, crunching it to a ruddy paste, and swallowing it. Down it took its alimentary way. She so burned with desire that her rectum bubbled with molten gold.

Pan flipped Adrasteia onto her belly and eased his erection up her ass, the liquid gold a lubricant that at nearly two thousand degrees Fahrenheit would have fried a mortal dick to nothing.

But Pan endured the fire with ease. Into it he shot his immortal spunk. When he withdrew, out spilled a stream of gold-foiled chocolate coins.

"At last, I have you back."

But when she turned her head toward her lover, he was gone.

Henceforth, before each evening's visit to children's bedrooms, the Tooth Fairy replayed in imagination of exceptional vividness her sex with Pan. She thought it real, and to her it was.

On her rounds, she likewise imagined that she was finally able to bring her hatred for little boys and girls to bear on their helpless bodies.

Truth was, she had never been more genuinely kind and loving to every child. But in her mind, she ripped them apart, painting their bedrooms in blood, gore, and spews of pulverized bone. She tore back the scalp flesh and swallowed their skulls. Their pitiful remains she buried in a voluminous clatter of shat coins.

Would this pooped-out embarrassment of riches encourage Mom and Dad to spawn more rug rats?

If it did, why, all to the good. More post-toddlers to snuff out on future house calls.

At the next tooth loss, she would find the same child all over again, blind as she was to the illogical erasure of her past bouts of mayhem and murder.

Thus she lived out her days.

Upon returning to the island, the Tooth Fairy truly had the upper hand with her imps, the control totally hers now, and they kept their distance.

They suspected the truth about her visits.

A few careful trips by Cagger and Clunch—Gronk was too freaked to go himself—soon confirmed their suspicions. But they feared her ferocity and did not dare try to enlighten her.

She was content with her delusional daily sex-bout with Pan, imagining herself triumphant at last over his absurd wives, having him, loving him, devouring him, fucking him and letting him fuck her whatever way he liked.

Life was grand.

And she was in charge.

There was one small flaw in the Easter Bunny's new life—or the pretense at one—of familial bliss. That flaw had three parts.

Fake fuckmate Petunia.

Fake cute bunny offspring.

And an illusory set of cock and balls.

It was true that having borne witness to the more than seven billion fucks of Aphrodite and Saint Nick had changed him for the good.

His voyeurism had turned to witnessing. His eyes were holy as he viewed the marvels of mortal fucking. And the twitch of his nose continued to bring about a healthy pregnancy in any couple that truly desired it.

What then the flaw?

First, he regularly—as in every night—dreamt that he was alone in his burrow. In dream, Petunia and the little fluffy bunnies were not real, not at all. They were a delusion meant to ease his loneliness. Moreover, the magnificence of his genitals—the heft, the erections, the abrupt expulsions of bunny sperm—weren't real either. In truth, he was smooth down there, his lovely package wiped away for an unpardonable sin he had committed not so very long ago.

But every morning, he opened his eyes, shook his darling Petunia awake, had his way with her and she with him, and showered oodles of fatherly love on his offspring.

Silly dream!

Still it held power over him, recurring, refusing to leave him alone.

And that sin?

Rape.

The sin for which there was no forgiveness.

He let it sit, slumped, in the corner. It never lost its stench. He had changed radically over the last many years, had grown good and useful, had helped Santa and Wendy save the human race from extinction.

But yielding to an urge to violate mortal women as a means of fighting loneliness—and then raping Rachel to curry favor with the Tooth Fairy—that would always be part of his past.

Deflated.

Estranged.

Forever defiled.

There was no way around it, no way to be washed clean, no way to reverse those violations. He had to content himself with preparing his annual deliveries around the globe and with enjoying his happy family in his off hours.

But his moments of solitude before dinner each day, hopping about the woods outside his burrow—these were moments of deflation, steady, reliable, sobering.

And in this deathless immortal life, he would never see an end to them.

The following Christmas Eve was like no other that had gone before. It bristled with vivid reds and greens and whites. And with the aromas of holly, eggnog, and apple cider, of pine and spruce brought indoors and decked with tinsel, ornaments, and bright lights.

But oh my, the sounds. The jingle of bells. Rich new carols woven about the old standards. Words of grace and good will in every land in all languages. A blessed silence where the din and yammer of commercialism and greed had so recently held sway.

In response to the pleas of Santa and his family and co-workers, the Father God had made magic time far more extensible. After all, the Nice list now included every child on the planet. The Naughty list was a thing of the past. And so, a vast abundance of gifts had to be made and delivered. There were more homes to visit, more milk and cookies to be consumed, more carrots to feed to Lucifer and the other reindeer.

Santa and Wendy looked in on many boys and girls dozing in their beds. Even in sleep, there was an aura about them, a new peace and calm. This was finally a blessed race of creatures indeed.

Grown-ups who were childless—couples or loners, widows and widowers—stayed up much of the night in revelry.

And that revelry no longer confined itself to one religious tradition. Instead of merely a celebration of the Christ child's birth, it became a celebration of new birth in all people, no matter their age.

They were out and about, hymning the universe in true fellowship. Their songs were spontaneous. They went about with faces that spoke marvels at what had happened since Valentine's Day.

Fear had lifted from their shoulders. No longer were there causes to justly fear.

No soldiers, no cops, no guns.

No thieves, no greed, no prisons.

No fistfights, no rapes, no murders.

No hate, no hunger, no neglect.

Santa went from one joyous home to the next. The difference between this year and last was dramatic. Where once the home of Rick and Sandra McFee of Union, New Jersey had been steeped in gloom and sorrow, now it bubbled over with love and joy, with grace and gratitude. Their bratty sons, Billy and Max—budding sociopaths both—had turned into little saints, well deserving of the toys Santa set beneath their tree.

Wendy too laughed all night, bringing each blessed boy and girl on board her sled, showing them some of what lay ahead in their futures. Bright futures all, now that confident and competent grown-ups encouraged them to learn, bend, then break rules, reforge swords, find their unique voices, talents, and forms of joy and generosity.

There was much to talk about when they returned to the North Pole.

And talk they did, through the night and into the next day's festivities. Rachel and Anya sat enthralled, as did the elves, at the tales they told.

One other change should be mentioned.

In large part, this change came about from Santa's scheduled liaisons with Aphrodite. There in her bower, through their more than seven billion love-fucks prior to the Great Transformation, followed by the three and a half million love-fucks per week for newborns, Santa seamlessly integrated his Pan self.

As a result, Santa's lovemaking with his wives took several quantum leaps in sensual expertise. They loved in equal measure his gentleness and roughness. Their sex became playful, vigorous, probing, ever new, ever inventive. It often lasted weeks of magic time, surging ceaseless as the sea, salty, full of power, restful in its restlessness, rich with new life below, its surface shining with sunlight, moonlight, and the light of distant stars.

As for the elves, they picked up on Santa's change and ventured into more open sexuality themselves.

Their annual days of frolic on and near the snowy commons right after the Christmas delivery turned into a Saturnalia—an ecstatic union with the divine—especially now that female elves had been introduced into their community.

On those days, even more than the rest of the year, they switched partners. And impromptu orgies in the commons—snow flying wildly everywhere—had been added to their traditional snowball fights and to their exuberant play on the skating pond.

The only elf who refused to switch sex partners was Gregor. He had always hidden himself away on those days, scowling at festivity and sensing that he would be mercilessly buried in snowballs were he to show his face outside the stables.

As for the others, they stripped on a whim, grabbed the first—and sometimes the second or third—willing partner, and humped right out in the open, making the most astonishing snow angels anyone had ever seen.

As quickly, they would shake off the snow—using it to wash away the fluids from their bodies, inside and out—suit back up, and join the snowball fight always in progress.

None of these activities suffered discontinuity.

All of them were expressions of joy, of life zestfully lived, of the playfulness of physical embodiment.

On those days of Saturnalia, elves coexisted easily with satyrs and wood nymphs. Displays of affection, of adoration, of brisk and welcome ravishment were the order of the day.

Watching from their porch, Anya felt conflicted. For she recalled her days as a pine nymph, indiscriminate pairings and pluggings, the joys that went with divine intoxication, not a care in the world, all the necessities provided for them and no predators of any kind. She could see and identify each satyr, each wood nymph, and recall vividly her lascivious matings in those days of old.

Longing rose in her for recouplings of the same sort in her new guise as Santa's wife. But she held onto her station, confided in Rachel and Claus, and brought her fantasies into their lovemaking each night, driving the threesome higher into ecstasy.

Santa, feeling obliged to be the jolly old linchpin, held back from abandoning himself to sex play in the commons. Still, he had a heartfelt desire to enjoy the female elves on a regular basis. Oh, not in their huts, not as elves, but as tree nymphs, chasing them in his Pan persona through the woods and taking them in the throes of a drunken frenzy.

But he managed to suppress his desire and content himself with the paradise he had been granted. Chuff stood by his side much of the time, looking confused at the orgiastic goings-on, a good-natured dolt of a fellow and as hard-working as any elf. Wendy linked arms with Adonis, too modest both of them to share their sexual connection in so public a fashion.

Joy filled the healing earth as it spun upon its axis, nowhere more so than at the northern tip, that place of magic where saint, elf, satyr, nymph, and reindeer dwelled in perfect harmony.

EPILOGUE
THE ELEVATION OF A SAINT

One night in Santa's office, the Son dropped by.

Together, they lamented the Father's decision to abandon Santa's perfected under-psyches, reverting to His old flawed model instead.

"Maybe I can talk Him into using them. I can work on Him, try to change His mind."

"Wouldn't that be lovely?"

Then a look most engaging, and engaged, crossed the jolly old elf's face. Visions of Aphrodite, no doubt, and the delightful measures required to maintain the health of the human race, one Sunday at a time.

"But I'd sure like it—in fact I'd be eternally grateful and I mean that quite literally, Rachel and Anya too—if you could delay your persuasive efforts."

The Son laughed and promised he would.

Eventually, though, he started in on the Old Man.

"Dear Father, You might want to consider," he said, "taking a more careful look at Saint Nicholas's under-psyche. The craftsmanship is superb."

God's face turned crimson. "What's wrong with My model?"

The Son wisely refrained from reeling off an endless list of botches. "Nothing, of course. It's served us well for ages."

"Indeed it has."

"That said, if You were to find merit in one or two of Santa's alterations, wouldn't my delivering them—and a few physical improvements thrown in as well—make for a bang-up Second Coming?"

The Son detailed what those improvements might be. God perked up. "We'll see."

That was as close to a yes as the Father ever came in such

163

matters. So the Son changed the subject. "Things turned out well, don't You think?"

"They did."

"Catastrophe averted."

The Father glowered at him. "Yes, though not by Me. In fact, in spite of Me. That's what you're trying to say, isn't it?"

"You were very naughty, weren't You, Father?"

"I was. Shame on Me." He gave Himself a light swat on the back of the hand. "There."

"Father, do You think that's sufficient punishment for doing what You tried to do?"

In reply, God flicked a finger at his Son, hurled him back onto a blazing cross high up in the heavens, and multiplied his suffering a hundredfold.

For eternities of exceedingly drawn-out magic time, He left the Son hanging there in agonies of pain. Then He wrenched him from the cross and threw him down onto the floor of the Empyrean.

The crucified one looked worn and haggard, doing his best, but failing, to come to his feet in front of the throne.

"No question in my mind, Son. Not the least scintilla of doubt. Do you agree? Well do you?"

One moment, Santa was on his evening walk with Wendy. The next, he found himself standing before Almighty God.

The Son lay nearby, grimacing in pain.

"Are you all right?" Santa bent to help him up.

"Resting, Nicholas, that's all. I'm okay."

"Liar," said God. "Pay him no heed, Santa. Let Me pay him heed, in spades."

God glowered at the Savior.

"Listen up, you stupid, insufferable boy. Your First Coming was an utter failure. Your followers, and the insane fanatics that came after, slapped together an exclusionary religion. You failed to see that coming. You made ambiguous statements you ought to have known might lead—given the perversities of mortal nut jobs, nincompoops, and just plain Christ-fucking assholes drawn to the security of a cult—to such an outcome. You failed to warn with sufficient sternness against that."

"But Father, such people no longer exist, thanks to Santa, Wendy, and the Easter Bunny."

"And no thanks to you!"

Santa Claus stood aghast.

"Now then, saintly one," said God, turning the full radiance of His countenance upon Santa, "let's talk about why I've summoned you."

"By all means, but—"

"O thou jolly generous bestower of gifts, I hereby make you my second son, on an equal plane with this fellow here."

At His words and the nod of His great head, Santa felt a glow rise from his toe tips up his legs and thighs, crisscrossing at his groin and sweeping up through his jelly-bowl belly and his barrel-of-jellybeans chest into his neck, his chin, his cheeks, his nose, his forehead, right out to the tippiest tip of every last snow-white hair on his head.

A halo encircled that head, which halo Santa could see and feel entire, as though he were outside himself.

He felt . . . elevated.

And with that sense of elevation came a new clarity about what was what.

As if for the first time, Santa saw clearly the failure of God to be a competent, not to mention a superb, creator. There stood out the changes that had failed to stick: the command that mortals be polyamorous, and the only-temporary eradication of homophobia which had surged stubbornly back.

The Almighty seemed incapable of overcoming the inertia He had himself created.

Santa saw too the new human race. It amazed him how swiftly they were becoming realized beings.

Regrets still abounded among mortals. Temptations too, and sorrows, though all of them were muted and now finally easy to control.

Their psyches were at last whole and functioning as well-engineered psyches ought to function.

Even so, there was death. There were accidents that

crippled and maimed. Illnesses and allergies, viruses and bacterial infections, food intolerances and ways to compromise the immune system—these continued to plague humankind.

Bereavement still hurt.

He fixed on a man just turned sixty-six in northern Colorado who had lost his wife of seventeen years to fallopian tube cancer. A year had passed and still the man kept his wife's clothes and all her papers, her art supplies in the basement, her rings and bracelets and earrings organized in practical boxes in their master bedroom, just as they had been at her death. He had lost what he had relied upon to help define himself. So sad it was to feel his grief, this man who had once been such a well-behaved child and who had been a fairly well-behaved man, all things considered.

Then Santa pulled back and took in all the men and women lost in bereavement. Grievers freshly minted, grievers incapable of letting go, and those about to be stricken with grief.

His work on the psyche had addressed, at long last, self-generated problems. But physical woes were still present and active in their lives.

He had to find a way to deal with those woes, either through the Second Coming or some other way.

But Death was the biggie. That was clear.

Yet death must surely be reversible. After all, Rachel and Wendy had died and been resurrected. Why, he himself, once seemingly dead, had been restored to life.

As Santa, as Pan, and now as a newly minted son of God the Father, he ought to be able to deliver this gift to the human race.

There had to be a way.

Then doubt surged in.

"Oh, but dear God in heaven, I have my hands full with overseeing the making of toys and their delivery. How could I possibly take on—?"

God laughed.

"Fear not, jolly one. It's an honorary title only, at least so far."

He sniffed at His first son.

"However, when it's time for the Second Coming, you might be the one I choose to send on that mission, not this joker here. He pretty badly botched the First Coming, didn't you, sonny boy? And Santa, you've got quite the track record for succeeding at any task that's tossed in your lap."

Santa started to object.

"Let's have none of that!"

He shut his mouth.

"In the meantime, be open with your desires. I sense there's one unspoken. Say it. No, wait. I already know it, of course. Just a moment."

In an instant, Rachel and Anya had joined them and God took the three of them aside.

God spoke Santa's deepest desire. Santa, alarmed, suffered a twinge of angst. No way would he have stated it so frankly, for fear of alienating his wives.

But the Almighty had a way with words.

"I think we can agree to that," said Anya.

Santa sensed hesitancy in her words.

Rachel was far more enthusiastic. "Our sex life has been greatly enhanced by our husband's trysts with Aphrodite and even his one last fling with the Tooth Fairy. Why shouldn't the same be true in this case?"

"Quite right," said Anya.

Rachel went on. "But are You sure it won't disrupt their—"

"Toy making? No, dear lady. Pan and his nymphs will retain vivid memories but at a millionth the intensity of the romps themselves. No lingering distractions, then. None at all."

The Father returned the women to the North Pole.

Too easy, thought Santa. I'll have a heart to heart with them both before too long.

"Every night, just before you climb into bed, you will enter magic time and be transported here—"

The Father gestured earthward. Through the eyes of Pan, Santa saw the re-creation, at a remote corner of the North Pole, of his favorite stomping grounds from Greece. Pine, ash, and

167

poplar. Soft moss carpeting the ground, ideal for a horizontal lay, moist with a dew so thick it would be ideal for lubricating those hard-to-enter orifices.

"—and here you and your tree nymphs will indulge your wildest lusts, go drunk on wine and flesh, savor every delight, taste every sensual joy."

"But how does this tie in with my usual—?"

God flared. "You two have got to respect your Old Man, learn humility, trust your daddy's judgment."

A new confidence surged through the jolly old elf.

"I respect You entirely," he said. "I always have and even more so now, as Your new-created son. Forgive me, then, this tiny gesture."

With that, Santa, moved by compassion, lifted the Son to his feet.

"You will stop that."

Santa continued.

"I command you."

With neither disdain nor defiance, Santa ignored the Father God's command.

The Son's gratitude, full upon Santa's face, shut out all else from his mind.

"This is your final warning, Saint Nicholas!"

And for a long time afterward, no more words came from the mouth of God.

ABOUT THE AUTHOR

Robert Devereaux made his professional debut in Pulphouse Magazine in the late 1980's, attended the 1990 Clarion West Writers Workshop, and soon placed stories in such major venues as Crank!, Weird Tales, and Dennis Etchison's anthology MetaHorror. Two of his stories made the final ballot for the Bram Stoker and World Fantasy Awards.

His novels include Slaughterhouse High, A Flight of Storks and Angels, Deadweight, Walking Wounded, Caliban, Santa Steps Out, and Santa Claus Conquers the Homophobes. Also not to be missed is his new short story collection with Deadite Press, Baby's First Book of Seriously Fucked-Up Shit.

Robert has a well-deserved reputation as an author who pushes every envelope, though he would claim, with a stage actor's assurance, that as long as one's writing illuminates characters in all their kinks, quirks, kindnesses, and extremes, the imagination must be free to explore nasty places as well as nice, or what's the point?

Robert lives in sunny northern Colorado with the delightful Victoria, making up stuff that tickles his fancy and, he hopes, those of his readers.

You can find him online at Facebook or at www.robertdevereaux.com.

deadite press

"Earthworm Gods" Brian Keene - One day, it starts raining-and never stops. Global super-storms decimate the planet, eradicating most of mankind. Pockets of survivors gather on mountaintops, watching as the waters climb higher and higher. But as the tides rise, something else is rising, too. Now, in the midst of an ecological nightmare, the remnants of humanity face a new menace, in a battle that stretches from the rooftops of submerged cities to the mountaintop islands jutting from the sea. The old gods are dead. Now is the time of the Earthworm Gods...

"Earworm Gods: Selected Scenes from the End of the World" Brian Keene - a collection of short stories set in the world of Earthworm Gods and Earthworm Gods II: Deluge. From the first drop of rain to humanity's last waterlogged stand, these tales chronicle the fall of man against a horrifying, unstoppable evil. And as the waters rise over the United States, the United Kingdom, Australia, New Zealand, and elsewhere-brand new monsters surface-along with some familiar old favorites, to wreak havoc on an already devastated mankind..

"An Occurrence in Crazy Bear Valley" Brian Keene- The Old West has never been weirder or wilder than it has in the hands of master horror writer Brian Keene. Morgan and his gang are on the run--from their pasts and from the posse riding hot on their heels, intent on seeing them hang. But when they take refuge in Crazy Bear Valley, their flight becomes a siege as they find themselves battling a legendary race of monstrous, bloodthirsty beings. Now, Morgan and his gang aren't worried about hanging. They just want to live to see the dawn.

"Muerte Con Carne" Shane McKenzie - Human flesh tacos, hardcore wrestling, and angry cannibal Mexicans, Welcome to the Border! Felix and Marta came to Mexico to film a documentary on illegal immigration. When Marta suddenly goes missing, Felix must find his lost love in the small border town. A dangerous place housing corrupt cops, borderline maniacs, and something much more worse than drug gangs, something to do with a strange Mexican food cart…

"Jack's Magic Beans" Brian Keene - It happens in a split-second. One moment, customers are happily shopping in the Save-A-Lot grocery store. The next instant, they are transformed into bloodthirsty psychotics, interested only in slaughtering one another and committing unimaginably atrocious and frenzied acts of violent depravity. Deadite Press is proud to bring one of Brian Keene's bleakest and most violent novellas back into print once more. This edition also includes four bonus short stories:

"Whargoul" Dave Brockie - It is a beast born in bullets and shrapnel, feeding off of pain, misery, and hard drugs. Cursed to wander the Earth without the hope of death, it is reborn again and again to spread the gospel of hate, abuse, and genocide. But what if it's not the only monster out there? What if there's something worse? From Dave Brockie, the twisted genius behind GWAR, comes a novel about the darkest days of the twentieth century.

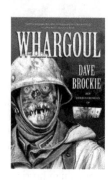

"Highways to Hell" Bryan Smith - The road to hell is paved with angels and demons. Brain worms and dead prostitutes. Serial killers and frustrated writers. Zombies and Rock 'n Roll. And once you start down this path, there is no going back. Collecting thirteen tales of shock and terror from Bryan Smith, Highways to Hell is a non-stop road-trip of cruelty, pain, and death. Grab a seat, Smith has such sights to show you.

"Apeshit" Carlton Mellick III - Friday the 13th meets Visitor Q. Six hipster teens go to a cabin in the woods inhabited by a deformed killer. An incredibly fucked-up parody of B-horror movies with a bizarro slant
"The new gold standard in unstoppable fetus-fucking kill-freakomania . . . Genuine all-meat hardcore horror meets unadulterated Bizarro brainwarp strangeness. The results are beyond jaw-dropping, and fill me with pure, unforgivable joy." - John Skipp

AVAILABLE FROM AMAZON.COM

deadite press

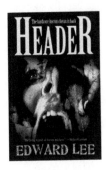

"Header" Edward Lee - In the dark backwoods, where law enforcement doesn't dare tread, there exists a special type of revenge. Something so awful that it is only whispered about. Something so terrible that few believe it is real. Stewart Cummings is a government agent whose life is going to Hell. His wife is ill and to pay for her medication he turns to bootlegging. But things will get much worse when bodies begin showing up in his sleepy small town. Victims of an act known only as "a Header."

"Red Sky" Nate Southard - When a bank job goes horrifically wrong, career criminal Danny Black leads his crew from El Paso into the deserts of New Mexico in a desperate bid for escape. Danny soon finds himself with no choice but to hole up in an abandoned factory, the former home of Red Sky Manufacturing. Danny and his crew aren't the only living things in Red Sky, though. Something waits in the abandoned factory's shadows, something horrible and violent. Something hungry. And when the sun drops, it will feast.

"Zombies and Shit" Carlton Mellick III - Twenty people wake to find themselves in a boarded-up building in the middle of the zombie wasteland. They soon discover they have been chosen as contestants on a popular reality show called Zombie Survival. Each contestant is given a backpack of supplies and a unique weapon. Their goal: be the first to make it through the zombie-plagued city to the pick-up zone alive. But because there's only one seat available on the helicopter, the contestants not only have to fight against the hordes of the living dead, they must also fight each other.

"All You Can Eat" Shane McKenzie - Deep in Texas there is a Chinese restaurant that harbors a secret. Its food is delicious and the secret ingredient ensures that once you have one bite you'll never be able to stop. But when the food runs out and the customers turn to cannibalism, the kitchen staff must take up arms against these obese people-eaters or else be next on the menu!

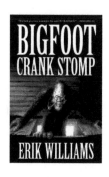

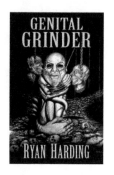